TRISHA NIHARIKA

Intense

BLUEROSE PUBLISHERS
U.K.

Copyright © Trisha Niharika 2024

All rights reserved by author. No part of this publication may be reproduced, stored in a retrieval system or transmitted in any form or by any means, electronic, mechanical, photocopying, recording or otherwise, without the prior permission of the author. Although every precaution has been taken to verify the accuracy of the information contained herein, the publisher assumes no responsibility for any errors or omissions. No liability is assumed for damages that may result from the use of information contained within.

BlueRose Publishers takes no responsibility for any damages, losses, or liabilities that may arise from the use or misuse of the information, products, or services provided in this publication.

For permissions requests or inquiries regarding this publication, please contact:

BLUEROSE PUBLISHERS
www.BlueRoseONE.com
info@bluerosepublishers.com
+4407342408967

ISBN: 978-93-6452-641-8

Cover design: Daksh
Typesetting: Tanya Raj Upadhyay

First Edition: December 2024

CHAPTER ONE

My heart is breathing very fastly there is a kind of comfortness but also little bit of anxiety. I knew him for years before we got so close before. Damn I was waiting for him, I was really wanting to see him really badly, he texted me he will come and see me this afternoon. But I wasn't sure that he will be coming …There is a kind curiosity in my mind that may I will be able to see him. Its a Saturday afternoon, I have dimmed the lights, my room is little bit cozy with yellow lights, I know its afternoon but I have put all my curtains, so that room can be little bit warmth and cool. Saurav always wanted the room to be little bit dark, he wants little bit of coziness I know and he don't want sun rays on his face, I liked this kiddish behaviour of his. Lights was dimmed, he called me I reached. I told, "Come up, I am in my room only just informed the guard that's all."He came to my room and hugged me after so many days.

He is so young, tall, handsome, attractive, charming, good -looking, dressed in a white T -shirt and a dark shade black denim jacket on it, with a blue denim jeans and a dark black hair with little bit of smile, he is wearing a pair of specs which enhances him to look little serious. He is really tall from me when he hugged me he laughed and said, "Esha you are really short, too short, you don't come to my chest also. Thodi toh height bana lo "He asked me for a glass of water and told," You sit I want to freshen up little bit ", I was just calm and little bit shy, it happens I guess when someone you like is with you, you become little bit of shy otherwise I am a bold personality. I opened the fridge took out some cold water and mixed it with some normal, one he always wants 50 /50 everything mostly he drinks water or anything, he likes it to be little bit of warmth. I was tired so I just went to bed waiting for him to come so that we can chit chat its long time, we did not spoke to each other for so long. My bed was having a floral dark brown print on it, he laughed slightly, and told, "Your love for florals is never gonna end soon I guess". I replied," Off course". I laid down in bed just took the support of his chest. I laughed and told you took all my lighters, I know you take my things with you everytime you come and see me. He smiled very cutely, and told ya I got one for you. He took out a red lighter from his pocket and burnt one cigarette. He is having habit of cigarettes from college days and I know this so for him I always smile. I told, "Saurav bring your own ash tray na.." in a typical bangalorean way. I get irritated because of this, he always uses my utensils as an ash tray, but he smiled and told, "I am not using your's utensils, its mine". His intense look sometimes gives me gooosebums, I laid in bed, hearing his office problems and how he is just tired of all those stuffs. He wanted to sleep next beside me, he spoke to me how much he is tired, his whole week was little bit of tiring and he wanted to talk about "us". There was so many reasons for us not to be together long back, but I could see in his eyes that he is so sorry for not being there for me and the only thing that I could see in his face was the willingness of being one.

For an Indian boy expressing his feelings is not so easy but what I like about him is the way, he doesn't feel shy about expressing his thoughts, words and emotions, its really commendable that he is being real.

I was resting in bed while, he was smoking and talking to me, he was little bit sensitive while talking to me, as there was a time gap between us when we last met and talked like that. He came beside me, hugged me very tightly and told me how much he missed me during those days.

"I was in left side of bed he hugged me from back, on first it felt me ashamed off and shy, he just wished to be with me, be close to me and rest with me. He gently kissed me on my neck from back, I felt like someone is tickling me, at first I did not like it, as it was too sudden for me. He asked me, "Are you comfortable with me? Because I have not seen him since months, there is a sense of discomfort for me to be with him, sometime there is a kind of discomfort or sense of distrust which arise when u don't see someone for days, and when some people make you think negative about someone, though attraction is there, it's a kind of trust issues, may be that person is not with you that's why but actually the problem is within us. If you really like a person, the tension should not be because of us but rather than us we think of other person's stressed first.

What comes in mind first is the problem what is in his mind. I was passionate about my feelings for him but one thing which was stopping me from getting too close is not that I don't like him but it's the fear of losing him. This tension of losing him might seem a very small issue but it is not a small issue rather it's the most terrific thing I could ever feel in my life. Looking at his eyes, made me weak, that I could not stop loving him, in our last meeting he explained about not being together as he is leaving for Pune and it will be difficult for him to be far from me. So, we both took a serious step of not getting to close with each other. But destiny has its own choice, we spoke about our lives, he told me about his concern of not being together is Mayank, I don't know how to react to this, he is my ex, which means I have moved on, we are mutual friends so he was scared that Mayank might be offended with our relationship.

"Damn SAURAV is this the time to talk about this right now, I know Mayank was with me till today I respect him and you have to understand that I respect him the most in my life but I choose you please try to understand "I told, I could not control myself I hugged him. It was intense moment, I want to kiss him but I was controlling myself, everything was calm, room was dimmed, it was almost for a person to kiss but I was not moving forward, as he did not wanted it. He hugged me tightly, and started to cry, he wished to be with me I could see this in his eyes. I asked, "What is stopping you tell me I will try to figure it out ?" He said, "Esha please don't make things worse for me ", He told "I am leaving to Pune for work, I'll be back after some days, he explained we should not meet so frequently, it's a kind of disturbance to him. For his willingness I told,

"Okay, I'll see you then", he was just leaving, he booked Rapido, it was on the way. He went to freshen up, as he was with me for many hours just doing chit chat and smoking and he was tired from all these tensions and stressed, he washed his face and came back. I told him to be to relaxed and not too take so much stressed what is the reason, he is smoking too much. While, he was in washroom, I was just combing my hair, as it was really little bit wet, as he just came to see me I took bath that time and could not dry my hair, so I was brushing off my water. He came near me, and spoke near my ears, "Good bye", with tears in his eyes but with a very intense way, I could sense it. He kissed me in my right side of neck, shoulders, he was smelling my body perfume,, he did not wanted to go I can strongly feel it. He was leaving, I touched his hands and told I want you to hug me tightly please, before you just go please. I don't know I was feeling that he might not wish to come back, there was a kind of mix emotions but something very deep and intense which I would have never felt before. He hugged me and kissed me on my forehead, my checks, from inside I was wishing not to leave me, suddenly the rapido called, he picked up and told, "I am coming Anna, just two mins ", I was opening my room door he was leaving, suddenly he cancelled the Rapido and came back and suddenly just kissed me in my lips. First time he did French kiss I thought he might made a mistake, he kissed me again, he in a hurry pulled off my shirt, I was wearing a light blue and white checked shirt with black shorts and black tan top, I could feel the passion in his eyes, passion for being together."Babe Go to bed", Saurav said. He opened his specs, kept aside near ash tray just beside my bed, came just near me, I touched him gently on his hairs I kissed his forehead, my eyes could not stop starring his eyes, for that moment I just wanted to live at present. He smiled at me, I could feel he is happy, he is so fair when the yellow light reflected on him for me it's the wish which was been granted. I told him, "Please don't stop". He sat with his knee in bed opened my tan top, my eyes were closed I was willing to bite his chest and lip. His hand is so gentle, he softly removed my top, slowly his fingers was at the back at my bras hook, I was feeling very shy though it was not our first time but whenever he touched me, my body becomes heated up. While he was opening by hook, my eyes was closed I could just feel it, he kissed me on my forehead, slowly could feel his lips biting my ears, he gently kissed my neck (feeling of so oneness), he did hickey just near my heart where my mole is it's so romantic, I stopped him wait, I bite his lip, I was touching his hair, it's really so smooth, I was having this in my mind that he is only mine and mine, I was tickling his chest, we both where two souls but one body. I could feel that he is just mine as a girl I always wanted that he stays with me always. I kissed on his chest, he was accepting that I'm there, I felt he always wanted that love from me. He was wishing this; he accepted the love what we both were making at that moment. I bite his nipples, I never did it before, I was crazy about him, he was telling me, "He is getting late he needs to go." "Don't think about anyone please babe, it's about us, Please don't think about anything, no work, no stress please, I just want you right now, I want us."I don't think so we should move forward" said Saurav."

"Please babe not now, please choose us before anyone else please. Right now please don't stop, I want you at this moment. I want you to fuck me right now, we have been waiting for this day I know please don't go Babe,."

I never call his name, I can't, for me he is only mine, I used to think, whenever he touches someone, I don't know, I wished he touches me with the most passionate way, with little bit of love, care, respect and sense of jealousy. We both were sleeping together, we both were kissing each other, his right hand was pressing my left boobs, I really wanted it."Keep going it, don't stop."Do you really want it, Esha?"

"I just want you, please". My hands was in his hairs, his lips was sucking my breast, I could feel his intensity (breathing heavily), he kissed me on my stomach, while pressing it, when his silky smooth hair touched my nipples, it's just a turn on for me."Are you sure?" I know we both wanted it, his fingers was opening my shorts, I was just loving his passion for me. I don't know when he kisses me, I don't want to stop (both tired)."We should not go further, I am leaving tomorrow."

"I don't want to be with anyone else now, damn fuck me na, please don't remove your hand, cause I wanted this. So listen to me, we want this". He hugged me(sighs), "I did not fuck anyone since 9 months, Esha no teasing, you are pushing every self control."

"Then what is controlling you, I will take everything on me." "I am sorry baby, I should leave, I can't do it, "Saurav said (with tears in his eyes with deep intense look) "Please leave right now Saurav everytime its about everyone, what about me, just go. Don't touch me anymore."

I stood up from bed, put on my clothes, "Just leave please, yes I think you should leave right now". "Baby listen to me, "he hugged me very tightly."Please listen to me, Esha, one side it's my friends, one side it's you, I am stressed yaar, please try to understand. I can't accept that you are Mayank's X, I don't I just can't."I gave his Huddie to him, "Wear it", meanwhile I booked Rapido for his home in Pai Layout.

"Listen to me yaar, stop it. Can you please just give me a second to explain please".

"I think you should leave from here, you have a flight tomorrow, go you should pack for tomorrow. No more talks now". My phone was ringing, I picked up, "Rapido madam". "Yes we are coming in just two minutes". "Saurav wear it, put your clothes on, you have to wear everything", he came to me, "Baby please listen na" (tears was in his face).

He was hugging me from back very closely, kissing on my hair, his hands was in my chest, consoling me "please". I was deeply upset, how much should a person should love, that the other person could sense it. How many time, how many years it will make someone understand that you really like them. It's just the attachment which really hurts, may be the person is not emotional but you feel as if you are having so much pain in your chest but you can't speak about it with anyone that deep down pain in your chest you cant express but still it makes you feel as if you have got a gun shot on your heart, the blood is just willing to come out but you are pressing it inside not to come out fast.

"Sometime you wish that person to be with you, that he don't go, I wanted to see him at last everyday, before he goes to sleep and I should be the first person to see him before he sees the sun, I just want whenever I'm standing in front of him, his hand should hold my stomach from back showing a sense of jealousy and showing sense of mine. His standing back does not mean he is weak, it shows that I am one and only his girl. I should be looking at him with a little bit of smile, while he is hugging his nephew, the intensity of my eyes should be so strong that I am happy that you are so caring. The specs what you wear is a serious look but it's the sense that you are serious and responsible at work, but when you come back hug me, I should open your specs and remove all your stress and keep aside. When you are with me, the stress that we both have at work should just vanish and we both are together making love more and more and this is how we grow together, personally and professionally and just being with each other for the years to come. I should be the first person who opens the button of your shirt and only I can wear your dark green shirt whenever I wish too, only my hand should touches your chest and I can keep my ears near your heart listening your high rate of heart beat and could kiss in your heart, only I can hold your hands in public. Looking at you makes me so calm and warmth that no matter what I know you are there |The sense that you will come back, the trust that you are mine, you won't leave, the hug you do takes away all my stress and responsibilities. I don't want anything from you rather than just you. Whenever you are with everybody just you think about me for a second no matter I'm with you or not, I am with you. At night when you sleep, just for a second you smile thinking about me how you feel while hugging me. Those charming smile of yours, it's something you see the world but for me I see you as my world, I am deeply in love with you Baby, I miss you, I always do, Please stay right now" I wish I could stop him.

He hugged me, his eyes was wet, he was just leaving, I could feel he will not come back, the strong sense was coming that I am sorry baby. I am sorry, we should not see again. I went down with him where the Rapido driver was there, I did not said a word, in my eyes I was just looking at him, maybe I'm seeing you the last time, and I won't be able to see you again. In my mind there was many things going on, he hugged me and smiled said, "Bye Esha". Those words I could here again and again its, been 14 days we last spoke up, these days for me it's just like a punishment for me as if I loved him, is by biggest mistake.

CHAPTER 2

It was 1st august 2016 chilly evening fresh air and the vibe is just, when I saw him first time, red and blue shirt check with blue jeans, wet hair, whispering with his school friends, gossiping about school, sitting at back bench how a 11th student would do just little bit of relaxing of the boards just get over, it's a new year for students and kids are just about to be adulting and this is the most happening and crucial for everyone as what subjects you might take after school, serious question like what you want to be ? What you see yourself about 5year later? But do you think we have thought about such a difficult question at those days, in the starting we all choose physics, chemistry, biology and mathematics for the safer side that at least get option and wide variety to go to college. Seriously, I took because I liked physics, chemistry and biology but mathematics is something that you like it or not but maths really loves us all. School was fun but then we realised we need to go tuition at 2:30 pm shit its Physics, Newton and Fluid Mechanics, these topic might leave us but Modern physics and Quantum theory is always with us.

I was sitting in front getting punishment of being late, I was wearing a blue floral printed shirt, with a blue jeans. Its my chemistry class at 6pm I just loved chemistry because nothing changes in chemistry, organic would be organic and non-organic cannot be mixed, I was really fascinated by the structure of molecules it was just like a solar system for me I could compare oxygen with moon as it's so beauty that everyone is attracted to it so much. I don't think anyone can hate chemistry, it will always make you love with it deep thinking and critical ideas. Adil sir, "Esha again late you sit in front only, why Beta? Now Don't' tell you are late because of Saurab sir. Everyone was laughing at me, it was all of friends only, they are all off my school friends. I looked back, I really saw him first time, he was smiling, laughing too loud, he was with Mrinal and Om, Rimanshu, his close friends but I did not knew because he was knew in class it was his first class, you could say everyone's 11th class new class but some of them was knowing me from 10 years, so they could relate me very much. At first I was angry on him, who is laughing at me, he does not know, but he was still laughing at me, others are my friends but he really don't know me but still laughing like we are too close.

The class was till 8:30, Adil sir, being Adil sir, he will extend class like anything, first he will say just this is last topic students we will end up soon, but he can extend till 10 pm everyone knew, he is like you all study we will eat dinner together. After class hats off to his confidence, he came to me and asked me I want your notebook, I am new I want to complete notes and he apologised for laughing at me too much. I asked him, "Do I know you how can I can give my entire notebook ? for so many days? Give me your number?" At first he thought I'm joking but after sometime, he said, "Really ?for this ?"

"Yes how can I trust a stranger? You might take it but send me your number so that I may remind you later on."He said "noted". My dad came to pick me up so, I left. I returned back home, just had dinner, I was at study table just nearly around 10 pm, reading for some more minutes.

A text message came, "Hi, Mayank this side". I replied, "Esha here."

We talked about each other for 2 hours just time passes. Then we realised that its late we have to go to school next day, so we stopped chatting and slept. Day next we did not met each other because I only met him on Chemistry classes which was on Monday, Wednesday and Friday from 6-8pm. I met him on Wednesday, I came again late, but for a surprise, he sat just at the back of me, the first second row was for girls only and then boys, I always sit at second row because I came little bit late due to my Physics classes which is from 2-4:45 pm, so ups downs for some minutes. At first, I got annoyed, that he was sitting just at my back because he was not my friend till then, we were just getting to know each other. I was different from him, he loved physics and maths and hated chemistry, but for me chemistry and biology were my favourite, physics also but maths little bit. Time passes, we came to classes, attended classes, studied and then went back home so these happened for about 2 months. One day my dad was getting late to come and pick me, I was alone standing, waiting for my dad and calling him, he told its going to be 20 minutes late due to work. Suddenly he came to me and asked, "why are you standing alone, let me drop you home ?". I asked, "No it's okay, I can wait for sometime".

"Okay but I will be here till your Dad comes, now Don't argue with me Esha."I smiled little bit "Okay fine". That was the first time, I noticed him, he has a really cute smile, he wore a blue T-shirt, he has an intense smiley eyes, his beard is little bit growing, he was growing to be a man, but at same time his innocence can be felt. His ears are little bit of long though, many friends called him, Manku due to his monkey, naughty behaviour. He was standing next to me to be surprise, he was shy, because at text he said what he felt but in front of me, he was little bit of scared. Because of my aura many boys get scared of due to my impression of being strict off course little bit of attitude and with a little bit of kind and humbleness. Mayank was always a talkative one, I always loved his shiny hairs, his dark complexion with long hairs was a perfect combination for a girl to have a crush on him. But for me till that day, he was only my friend but that day I really had a huge crush on him. He was just so sweet, he is a sakht launda kind of a boy, never ever he is going to show his emotions, it is clearly seen he was waiting at Hinoo main road where at night everything becomes chill and silent nobody is walking or moving but only because of me. He was just there for me without any expectations. I feel protected and safe for the first time in my life, I saw someone protecting me or thinking about me that much. I was elder sister at my home, so I was never used to such care and trust. He waited till my dad came, he said, "bye". I don't know, I went home eat dinner and texted him, "Are you alright? I know your dad might be angry at you, as you were really late today" I texted very late about 12:30pm. Mayank replied, "I am fine, Good night". I wrote, "I knew you had an argument with your dad of being so much late."At first, he rejected, then "Yes little bit of argument was there, my father told me to come back home, after tuition and prepare for IIT, don't mess with your future."I apologised, "I am sorry because of me…"

"Its okay Esha, see you at tuition."That night, he might slept but I was thinking about him, I was just fascinated by his behaviour, he stood up for me, I was really feeling more than just friends for Mayank. Many days passed by 11th finals came we talked little bit daily of our all where abouts and just was knowing more about each other. We were just so close friends we, were attached to each other so much that daily we were used to talk to each other, this happens for next 6 months. When we joined 12th class, we got separated our class timings got changed, but still we were connected to each other through calls and texts messages, meeting for tea and all. We were becoming best friends, knowing each other so much, it's the communication which both use to talk to each other about our day to day issues and whatever was giving us happiness it's all those small talks which was making us more and more closer.

For many days we could not talk as in class there was so much test going for competitive exams, that for some days we barely met due to boards, but still we did not saw each for months, this never separated us. Whenever I met him, I always felt that we met just last day, there was a comfort and bonding. I never felt awkward to talk to him though I met him after so many days. A year passed by, its Diwali time, he texted me, "Where are you I really want to see you?" I replied back, "At home but I am busy due to festival, I will try but I am not sure I can catch up with you this time". Actually from inside I did not wanted to see him, I was having tough days I lost one of my mentor and best friend some months ago, he died in an accident for me its losing one of the part of my life, I admired him, his energy of living a happy life always makes me smile, because of him I always wanted to be something and achieve success which will make everyone proud. He was a tall, fair skinned, having little bit of muscles as he joined gym recently, a cute looking guy who can be loved by anyone, but I was fascinated by the work he does, always working for the people, community and as a whole for all of us. He was doing MBA from Kolkata, he used to visit hometown on his holidays, he organises events, festival plannings and everything with a small group of people, he was a cheerful, fun loving person, who loves being with people, who is so much into organising and giving back to the society. Its Rishab, as the name sounds, he is just so cool calm guy who was loved and respected by everyone. I could see many times at family gatherings, he is alone cooking halwas for everyone at that time of pujas and he cooks with an open heart, he never expects anything from anyone I really respected him, for him it never came love, or like, I respected him, I always wanted to be like him humble, kind, generous whatever word comes in my mind will be suitable for him. To be honest he was an all-rounder, working to be good in athletics, playing guitar, being good in academics, he wanted to learn everything and he believed in transforming thing, his vision was really clear.

It was cool chilly night, at the time of December, when everyone was at home, he met everyone at his place and just informed us that he is going to meet his friends, and he will return home soon. We all were at his place; his all friends came to wish him new year. He was in a hurry he just informed everyone, "he is just going to drop Anil back home, and he will come back soon, you guys' takeout food, I am just coming back soon". His home was near railway station, the first right from the chowk, the white house two storeyed building is the "Siddhant constructions office, it is his home and office both. He took his i10 car I heard the voice of the gate that he opened and "please lock the gate Esha". The engine started, heard the horn, he went off. I went to lock the gate, as soon as I was returning back to table, I heard a thrashing sound, it was a huge crash, I could sense it, I thought someone had a tragic accident, I walk little bit on road, I saw nothing, I realised it might happen on the chowk itself at turning. Suddenly I was not feeling okay, it was something unusual, this pain what I felt, was same when I was a kid and I lost my grandfather then, who was my everything both mom and dad. I could feel that something is not right, the inside feeling was so painful, that I could feel it that my all the organs where just burning, it just very uneasy feeling, breathing problems just everything arises suddenly after some time, it was all chaos my friends came to me and said, "Let's go police called, take out the car, we have to rush". At first, I did not understand what happened. For me it was just upside down of everything. Just before some minute we were celebrating, and suddenly it does not feel right. Harsh and two of his friend rush to the hospital, the impact of mishap was massive. We rushed to the hospital, there was a corpse trolley, in which it was Rishab's body, he was tall, fair skinned, his death body was so discolorated, there was a bleeding from the nose, ears and mouth and his face was damaged, we could only see his body, his face was full of blood, there was a cut on his arms. I could just see blood on his body, it was so disturbing, it was a devasted accident, at midnight when everyone was sleeping, we saw our friend lying like a piece of skeleton and all his muscles was so stiffen. At hospital, everyone was calling him dead body, suddenly his identity was just changed from Rishab to a dead body. The police said, "We found him dead on driver's seat, he was full of bleeding nose, ears and mouth was just so broken out, we took his two injured friends to Medica where they are stable. The impact was too much in poles, and the metal shutter of the shop was too much damaged and shattered. This indicated that the car was being at high speed and too much rush was from drivers end. The crime scene was like that, Rishab saw a an auto coming from the opposite side, it was little bit of fog due to winter nights, he was going to crash with the auto driver, so he just took left turn he crashed to the pole, he lost his control, he was trying hard to control the vehicle he suddenly crashed to the metal shutter of the shop. He tried hard to control the vehicle as he was in driver's seat, he got more injured, he got stuck with the air bag of the seat, he could not come out from the seat as he was really 6. 8 feet he was really tall so it was i10 he could not able to come out of the car it was locked he tried but could not come out, he tried really hard to save his life but could not able to take his last breath. We could only save his two friends, we could not save Rishab, he was spot dead when we caught him, he was too injured, he was not breathing, no chance of saving his life, he went for eternal rest."We took his body home, we were Chistian so we had to get him buried the next morning. The whole hospital procedure was completed and the his body was discharged, the police allowed us to take the body and we can do the funeral as per the rituals. It was early morning we took his body home with the help of ambulance, everyone was crying in front of me, it was around 5am, when his mother screamed like anything, "Rishab please come back, what happened to you ", his sisters were crying everyone was shocked and screaming. The body was in the house, I could not understand how to react. I know crying could have been the reaction, but I could not react anything, I was just not ready for these things to happen. Sometimes you don't know how to react on certain situations, but the best is to just respond.

It was early morning we had got the timings about 12 pm for the funeral process the, Father had given the permission for funeral process cemetery, was there was people who had fought on war, it was greenery everywhere, it was looking as if I went to heaven, it was as if the rays was towards the cross.

As you enter the cemetery you will see all stones in triangular shape towards the cross, it's so beautiful, they have kept it so clean and memorable, it's the respect what people do to our soldiers, as the Father gave place at the after all the people were buried, we had got the last line, it was afternoon, it was started to rain, we took his body through van which which was decorated with his favourite white roses, we all wanted it to be peaceful. In Christian it is said that funeral should be done before 3PM, as it is having deep meaning, so at sharp

12 :30 it was going to be done, it started to rain, everyone was upset, mourning, my brothers Harsh, Raas, every brother took his body, came to the space where we have to bury him. When I saw that he is going forever, I could not see him, it was the time I really felt the pain, what the feeling was it could not be expressed, last night you saw him laughing wanting to eat dinner with you, and next morning I was burying him. He was cheerful person, just like us, had a dream to achieve many things in life, he was just so warmth and calm, staying with him makes you feel accepted, and his vibe makes the environment so comfy, and his presence makes everyone happy and joy. That was the time I could not stop crying, I was just so broken then from inside; I could not see him like never imagined that I am going to see him like this, then I started to realise that might be the last moment I am going to see him. I was not accepting what had happened, I was not ready to accept it, how anyone can accept it, the person you met last night, the next day you will not see him. Suddenly everything was up and down, my brothers were busy with the funeral process, everyone was crying but I was not able to process what had happened.

I had nothing to say, the person I respected the most had suddenly just vanished from my life. When you erase your writing on copy, it's so easy but when it comes to your life, everything just becomes difficult. When you are with that person, you never know what life is. When the whole process was over, everybody went back to home, I waited there, I don't know why I wanted to stay there for some time. It was just very calm, I could hear the birds chirping, as it was going to be sunset, at winters sun sets early. I was sitting next to the burial of Rishab, it was covered with white roses, candles, and hopes. I put the cross on his name, I shattered, I just couldn't believe what had happened, for me that was the time I couldn't express, I just can't explain anything, I respected him the most, I admired him but I want to do something which makes him happy. I still remember the smell of roses which I could smell, felt as if he smiles and he comes and say, "Kuhu bacchii kab badi hogi tum". I could feel his presence, suddenly I was feeling all empty, now I could feel lonely, I just felt lost what next, what should I do, I was very young, I don't know how to react, I was not so mature enough, I was just trying to accept what is happening with me, after my grandfather's death Rishab was my all-time favourite and now he is not with me, I could not process anything. I was just remembering him, and thinking I'll do what you wanted. I promised myself I'll live the gift of life, it is his life, I'll live to fullest, I know he is with me and he just wanted people to be happy because of him not crying at all. I went home attended the prayer meetings and all and I thought not to be upset but to live life what Rishab wanted, by this I can make him alive in my life and we will be always there with me, it's not that the pain will decrease or increase but I wanted Rishab's positive energy to be with me, just wanted him to be happy wherever he is and I'll respect his vision in my life always and always will be thankful that he came in my life for less time though but he was there and I will do what he might do to be living a cheerful and happy life. Till today its Rishab, whose smiley face so handsome that no one can beat him, his deep intense look person just so charming it's no words to describe him but rather just him, he will be always a cheerful baby doll to me.

Many days passed by, the life has to move on, I did not forgot Rishab but I tried to live daily in present because nobody knows what could be happening in future now. We can't change past, but always wish to work in present and change future. It was more than 6 months when Mayank tried to contact me but that time, my zone was really shocked and many things had happened till now so I really did not wanted to meet him, Why should I meet him, when I needed him the most, he was not there I was angry on him at first, I did not wanted to meet him really. Mayank wanted to see me, so I told him I can see you after Diwali, he accepted it and told "Okay but can you meet me before as after Diwali there are many pujas, so I might be very busy. So, I wish to see you before."He insisted so much that I could not rejected his offer, and said "Okay see you on Saturday afternoon"."Okay see you at 12 noon on Nucleus mall" he replied. The day of meeting him came to me and I was so calm I was trying to be mature enough so that our meeting does not get spoiled. It was afternoon, I was going to meet him for lunch, and then I had to pick my sister after school, my parents were working so I had to go and pick her up. I reached on Saturday afternoon at the time given by him, I reached before him, I called him, "Where are you? I had reached mall"."I am at lift Esha just coming you please wait; don't go I am just coming to food court". The food court was on the 4th floor I was waiting there standing in the edge at the balcony waiting for him, I was waiting near escalator so that if he comes, I can see him. I was on my phone just reading messages, when a suddenly a hand was kept on my shoulder, it was him, firstly I could not recognise him, for so many days I have not seen him so he got beard, he was little bit changed, he was not my Mayank it could be easily seen that he was not mine anymore. He was so happy to see me, his eyes was shining, he was just willing to talk to me so much that I could know this from the spark in his eyes. He told "Come sit", the whole food court was empty little bit it was 12 noon so not so busy, people were coming but its small town so at that time the place is empty little bit so though it was food court but it was not so crowded, so we managed to get two seats just near the glass edges so we could find a peace environment."Hii, how have you been Esha, how's life? I wanted to see you so much"."Ya

I am fine everything is okay, tell me about your life, I have not seen you from many days, I am just busy in my college stuffs" I replied."It so much to tell you babe, I have been in Bangalore these days just busy with college days, and you know na how much costly and expensive city Bangalore is, I had to buy movie tickets for 800 per person, so you can think that how much expensive it is and I have not came to Ranchi from many months and I came here so I wanted to meet you any how, I wanted to see you."He was so excited that he forgot to ask me how I am why didn't I called him, what could be the reason of mine not willing to see him, the love of my life till then. I knew him I wanted him to see me but at the same time I wanted him to ask how are you Esha from a boyfriends' perspective but he was not so matured till then. We talked for an hour, we ordered a red velvet cake and a tea, Mayank loved me so much that he never gave his food preference, but he always gives and buy whatever I liked. For me when I met him I just thought he came to me, when I was drowning in deep ocean, he just gave his hand and pulled me out of this drowning and pain in life. I forgot everything, every anger, every sadness, I loved his sparkling eyes and the intensity by which he loved me, everything just

vanished, I was just so happy to see him. That was the best Diwali gift he gave to me, that he came and wished me, he hugged me while leaving, he was so excited to meet me, and I was so overwhelmed to see him. It was my best time zones, after this meeting we became more closer, we started to talk day and night, Diwali went off and Christmas has arrived by that time I was in Delhi, time passed by it was March Holi had just got over. One day I just texted Mayank, "Baby I am coming to see you in Bangalore on 12th March 2022, I have a morning flight, I'll be willing to be with you this Holi time, I want you to fully fill my whole life with the colour of your love". At first he was shocked, as it was my first time I was going to see him in Bangalore, how he lives, who are his friends, and how he is? Is he sad or happy? More than him it's me who was excited to meet him this time, our relationship was going very cute, smooth, loving, everything was really going good and my career was also in full pace my studies was going on quickly and all together it was good. It was 12th march, I woke up 5am in the morning, I took bath with his favourite MCaffeine as I wanted to smell like coffee his favourite, I was super excited, my whole body was filled with goosebumps in every parts, my flight was going to depart from Indira Gandhi International Airport from 9:15 am and I was reaching Bangalore till 12 noon exactly. My journey started from Noida I was just willing to see him early morning happiness, I told him, "baby just reaching the airport, Good morning, I'll come till 12, Please come to pick me up on time, and be on time this time please."My whole flight journey was too much excited, though I should sleep for 2 hours but I could not sleep because I could imagine so many things on my mind, how is he, how will he react looking at me, is happy to be with me: more and more questions was coming in my mind. I was thinking it's the very long flight, 2 hours for me were as if I was looking for him with so many years, I wanted to be with him really. I reached Bangalore around 12 noon, I really was excited to see him, one of my friends had booked Gokulam Grand near BEL circle Bangalore -560054, for us, he was like "ja ja Simran ja ji le zindagi". I was very excited that I am going to see him, he was late, "Esha, you meet me directly to the hotel, I will be seeing you there, I have planned many things, we have to visit, you go freshen up, I am in traffic, I am on way coming soon". At first I don't know what to do, first time I came to Bangalore airport, and its different for me, I could hear people talking in Kannada and not Hindi, it was really weird for me, from whole childhood days, I have heard people speaking in Hindi, and suddenly, it made me panicked, how would I manage to go to Bel circle, it was 45 minutes from Airport and for me it was all so new, I never came to south before, it was all together new experience for me, I booked the uber, I was just growing and for me dealing things was really difficult, I was always protected and cared by my parents and friends that they never left me alone, so the worldly things seems to be so sudden for me. I somehow managed to reach Gokulam Grand, I was angry on Mayank as he was really late, he texted, "I am just reaching in 15 minutes, I went to reception and called him, "I am doing all check in you please just show your identity to the mam in reception and directly come to room"."Yes, baby I'll come you go bath."I did all the Check in all alone itself, and got room number 502, which was in the 5th floor itself, I wanted to get 11th floor but there was no room left as a wedding was going to take place at night so the whole hotel was decorated in such fresh flowers and the whole building was giving the vibes of happiness and joys and I was lucky to be a part of south wedding its really beautiful time, I could not wish anything more than this, I was having a person with me, whom I prayed to God each day that he should be with me for the rest of the life, Mayank was everything for me, he was my first love, the restlessness and the anxiety, and it was all about butterflies in heart, its true when you love someone, it's not about you, it's all about his happiness, I admired him the most, for me he was life, I can never see him hurtled or anything, its him always, that time my career was just starting, I was trying to manage work and him both, I just wanted we grow together, as an individual, and in all aspects of life. I thought we are a team, and we can fight the world all together. I went to the room, saw it was so white, only the furniture's where in dark brown colours, I was really excited, I was going to see him after so many days, I could not wait anymore, I went to bathroom while I was bathing I heard the doorbell, I understood it was him, "Oh shit I was not ready and he is here, shit how would I manage now, Esha do fast he is on way, he is going to come soon. I was just going to panic, the crush of my life is just going to reach soon, my anxiety level was on the top. The doorbell rang, I was just having mixed emotions I was going to see him, but I was scared to how he will react seeing me, I somehow managed and got ready with orange top and a blue jean with a black denim jacket. I saw him first he wore a white shirt with a green stripped on it with a blue jean, his hair was all wet, I could see him that he really rushed fast to come here.

I saw him he was always a cheerful person, he smiled, he was having little bit of beard, he was wearing a grey watch, how much a guy can be so handsome, whenever you will see him, his smile will make your day, he is just so talkative that he won't let you speak, his beauty is not in his face, but his honesty and his vibe will make you attract towards him, his long shiny hair, gives a compliment for him, he is just so honest and so focus that he always know what he wants in his life, I never saw a guy so focused on such a young age, he is inspiration not to me only but for all the one who he meets and work with them, he is just so serious towards his life. I spent more than seven years with him and I know how special he is to me, he is just like a water which should always flow, I just always want him to achieve whatever he wish too, his smile should always be in his face, I just don't want to see him upset, he is really a sunshine in my life, his rays of smile and happiness allows me to shine so much that in my face it's his thoughts and values, I have learnt a lot from him and wish to learn more and more from him in all the coming years. My most happiest part of life and also the bitter truth it's all because of him but yes the most important I respect him each day more and more; more than love I just respect him as an individual, his vision in life really teaches me how you should live life. Mayank is not just name in my life but it's my life, the life which I have is all because of him, when I was drowning in the ocean of depression and sadness, he was the one who just put his hand in water and made me come out from everything the anxiety and depression, today I live all because of him, the pain was in my life because of Rishab, it's all vanished because him. He is my medicine, the reason of my life, the whole evening which I waited to come so that I talk to him after a lot of work, what else I can say about the value he holds in my life. He is my pulse, my heart rate, my very force in my life, for as long as I breathe, the purpose of my life, he is my core, my heart beat of my body, he is my soul.

When I opened the door, I was shy and excited after seeing him, I told him to come inside. He came inside, sat in the chair just nearby my side, I was standing taking the back support of the work table which was all black, my whole room was little bit dark as I did not switch on the lights, it was all light yellow, and the curtains was in the shade of light brown, it was in the month of march so the heat waves was there in the morning, the ac was on so the room was not so hot but through the balcony the sun rays was fully coming inside the room through the glass panels that's why I had put the curtains so that room remains cold. He was very sleepy that I could see in his eyes, but he just saw me, he smiled and started saying, "Hi Esha, long time, how are you? I am sorry for being late, I was really stuck in traffic, I was not sleeping I was on time Esha"."Let me take rest till 4 pm wake me up then" (in a sleepy mood, my hair was all messy as I was inside blanket). I slept in a relaxed mood, I was in a deep sleep, suddenly I felt the hands of Mayank,

"Esha wakes up, you came from Delhi just to sleep baby, wake up (came to me gently kissed on my forehead) come let's go out for tea we will have something to eat, I am feeling hungry".

patience, my feelings was always, is wish, I never used to think about myself, the preference was first him always, but while I was growing with him, I was growing a lot learning new things like being patience, too much patient, too much caring for somebody else being less dramatic as he never liked when I did any kind of Dramas, he used to say, "Bas karo drama Esha". We both took auto from hotel to reach the New Bel road, Mayank used to come here with his friends so, he hang out mostly here, so he wanted to go to have some Dosa, so we went to his favourite Dosa place, it was really crowded, we somehow managed to get one table which is just on nearby one pillar, it was only we both so we managed, I told him,

"Sit Mayank you get dosa give me the bill, I'll get some juice for you". I always believed in equality whenever I saw him, I thought what much I can do for him, he is my friend, mentor, so I thought always whenever I got chance I try to help Mayank in every possible way, we sat there till 1 hour gossiping about everything, he asked about me and told me whatever was his life. At evenings, we walked at Bel circle, I could be with him anywhere, he is just best at smiles, his way of sharing everything me makes me realise that I am his everything, at night we came back to room, it was late 8 pm, we were sharing our daily live things, it was all just so happy whenever I talk with him, I could admire him my whole life, it was just getting late, I ordered cupcakes for him, I loved cupcakes, I told him, "Mayank please go and bring the delivery box, please |

It was all about friendship at first but then, it just got up closer and closer. He went down brought the food, I asked him, "Open it".

"Ya sure Esha", replied Mayank. I still remember, it was his eyes I was looking in, making him eat the cupcakes, I was deeply into his eyes, it was all late night, so I asked him to put the light off.

I guess he wanted me, but Mayank was never the one who will bump into me, directly to have sex but for him, being with me, listening me, just being around me was the most loving thing he always wish to do. He asked me, "Esha do you want the lights off?"."Ya babe just come near me and hug me."At first, he was shy it because for the first time he was so close and near me. He explained me how happy he was right at that moment, for me Mayank was making me so nervous, it was just so cozy night and being so immensely happy also but it was more of a making me just like that dream which was coming true but I don't know how to react it. I was continuously speaking, he kissed me and told shut up you cant say whole night babe. For me it was just goosebumps, Mayank was near me, making love but love is not about kiss or sex its all about just the respect, comfort and most importantly the trust what I have for him. We hugged and slept. I wanted to rest and so did he, we were more of a couple who was really boring though but the respect and closeness for us both was the most increasing and increasing day by day. The next day, at night I took flight back home, he came to the airport drop me home, and said, "Baby I'll see you after some days just be calm and you need to have some rest okay, I'll definitely catch you up later."

CHAPTER 3

Finally its so many years that we are together, I was excited really, I just thought I was making my relationship to another level, my best friend was going to be my partner, I was really feeling anxious, I was going to see him in Delhi, he shifted there so it was difficult really for me, as for me, Mayank is all about the whole, love, blossom, my habit, but when it's said everything is in right place, so maybe there is something which is really not right. I had a great time in December with Mayank so I thought Easter would be good surprise one, actually Holi just got passed and I really wanted two put my hands with colours on his face, I wanted his face to be covered with love of my happiness, hope for being together in life, it's not just a part of me but I never thought life without him.

I reached Delhi at evenings called him, "Hey babe, when are you going to be free, I am coming to your office we will have dinner together please"."Esha, I am working late little bit but I can try hard to meet you ", Why I came to Delhi, there is a reason behind it, for the past months there was things which was not going so good between us, there was lack of communication, lack of listening in between us we used to be so busy that we did not really was in touch so much, we both could not express ourselves with each other, what we were both going through, so I thought to surprise him, hugging from the back, just having both of us talking and sharing things with each other. He asked me to wait at coffee parlour near his office, I asked, "Mayank its going to be dinner time, I really wish to sit somewhere and see you from the nearest, want to be with you". I just wanted to impress him, so I asked him to reach at 8:30 PM so I have time to get ready, so I thought lets wear an Indian suit I knew green was his favourite colour so I thought I'll wear white floral printed suits but with his favourite green colour net dupatta which he really liked it, I put all efforts so that I may impress him, he might understands me that no matter any issues are there between us I am there Mayank I won't drop our relationship at any point of time, I'll figure it out, I will make everything and try to sort things between us and I will never gave upon us.

I just wanted him to know this that, for me I will never ever leave you, no matter what is going wrong between us I will make things better, the messed up life would be not just going to ruin us but I will try harder and harder to make this relationship work more and more. I know he was angry on me, for my behaviour of not understanding him, there was so much things in my mind that I want to talk to him, discuss about our problems, last night we had a serious fight, I could sense that he was really upset but as always I thought, Okay but we will again try to sort it down.

Mayank came from office, he was tired I could see, he was in his orange shirt with white lines on it with a black jeans I was waiting for him, for trying to solve things.

He came sat just in front of me,

I asked him, "How was your day Mayank, listen to me, I am sorry for yesterday and past days and for every issues, let's not fight babe, let's try to sort it na". He was not seeing me, his eyes could not see me directly; I could see it that he was trying hard not to look at my eyes something was bothering him a lot. I knew about his anger but I wanted to sort everything for him. He finished his favourite chicken noodles and chilli chicken, and he was enjoying his drink, he was ignoring me that I could sense it, he was replying his office mails at the middle of our talk(trying to portray as if he was super busy), he picked up his phone and told me, I am going for washroom, I will come back you wait here. He was just too upset with me, he did not wanted to see my face, I guess he had lost his patience on me.

"We both were here together till today everything was good (he explains with two palms together, he was very serious at that time), but I don't wish to stay together anymore, you can stay where ever we are but I really don't want to be with you anymore. I want you to move on, or you might stay there, I don't care, but I wish separation from you, I don't want to be with you anymore from now onwards."I could not take it at all ; I thought at least he would drop me home. I thought he would do it, at least I could have that much of respect left, but he booked an uber for me."Esha go home, you have a flight tomorrow you should go home its late night"

Mayank told. He came out with me, I thought what just happened, he booked an uber for me till metro station strange for me I thought maybe he could be with me some more time. We both waited outside till my uber came, there was a man, who was having a bike but he does one thing, waited for me asked Mayank, "Sir aap dono saath me ghar ja rhe ho, I would drop you both". Mayank in angry way, "Mam delhi jar hi hai and hum Noida me hai okay sir, Please drop her safely to metro station. I would be grateful to you please". I could see in his eyes a deep relief, he spoke to me, "I am feeling so much relief today, I am able to breathe now, for so many days I am not able to breathe in these tension, I am free now". I sat in bike, I was just really to upset, my tears can be seen pouring out as if the Mount Everest has just busted out due to excessive heat and climatic change, I was having a deep pain my chest, it was really paining a lot. On half way the Rapido bhaiya stopped and gave me handkerchief and asked me, "Mam aap thik hona ? I hope everything is okay, kya hua hai, kya kuch der ruke yanha two minutes, please breathe mam please".

In the whole ride I was just crying, there was tears in my eyes, that green dupatta what I wore for him, for him to touch and hug me was now the only dupatta left with the salt waters of my tears. I was shattered, I was just broken, my whole life was just upside down, I thought I lost everyone and everything in just few seconds ; him what I got back was somehow stolen from me, what was mine was no longer mine. I loved him, like anything and what I got, I heard this from him what in the whole world I can never ever hear this from his mouth. In metro somehow I called, Saurav he was my friend too I just asked him, "What happened with me Saurav, do you really knew about it ? Do you knew about all these things before? Why did you not inform me anything before, if you was knowing that this could happened to me". Saurav called me and told, "Esha, Mayank told me everything, where are you please come back home, please where are you yaar please don't cut the call, just be on call, please tell me where are you ? just tell me please. Don't harm yourself please."

I was crying, I lost the direction of my home, it was all raining, the paths were all wet and it was all dark nights my phone was having low battery, I was 12 am at midnight finding my route of home, I don't know everyone was just calling me Abhijeet just called me and told, "Esha where are you, call me where are you ?Did you reach home ? Where are you please pick up".

I somehow managed to reach back home, I saw Sakshi Dalal and Sakshi Yadav both was awake for me, they asked me, "Esha have you eaten anything, please tell na, we both are scared looking at you like this please"."Sakshi can you both sleep please I just want to be alone please for some time."I was in bed I was not talking to anyone I was just crying, my tears was not stopping that night. I guess never in my life I have ever cried that much, my life was all good, I never cried that much what I was doing that night. MY best friends both the Sakshi got scared they were feeling very tired but they could not see me like this, so they asked me, "please Esha sleep tomorrow we will see Tripti, then you board flight please sleep. That night I just got to know the true friends just be there with you went in bad times, I just don't know I was broken into pieces I have not ever thought that what I wished for is just scratched away for me. Some people don't think I am intense with my emotions because of the way I look and also the way I approach things with my brain always using never stopping, I am a overthinker, I just wanted things to be perfect and beautiful but did not realise that nothing is perfect it's the beauty of making things okay and accepting things the way it is. But actually I am just too emotional from inside I can't handle things especially when its about the person too close to me. I always wished that my schoolmate will become my soulmate for life accepting the separation of us was just shattering of my whole life, I can't express this with anyone us, I guess it will be in my life always the guilt of not being able to make things okay and better and I am just being sorry for not understanding him, its life I know but I know this will be with me till I die because it's the failure which hurts me more that one which should be the most important priority of my life I can't make it okay and fine, it taught me many things I am not perfect actually I am not okay for sure I have to change myself, learn many things to make things better in life personally and professionally both. This is something I'm sharing that I always wished that my love will be from school till my last breath I don't know partying away is always the most difficult thing which I could do, I did not knew many days have passed and still I don't know how to accept it, many months have gone but its still the same.

It's the same but I guess some people comes in your life suddenly without knocking the door, they just bump into your life without your consent and it really changes you, I was broken into small pieces that no one could fix ever, till a new character came into my life, How to describe him, it's funny that one person who just came into my life just give me the reason to live again and right now he is the only reason for me to learn and grow ahead in life, just accepting and understanding what went wrong and how to learn and forget things but learn each day with mistakes not only in career but altogether you are growing as an individual to be a better person. At the end it not just you, its what you make the change inside you and the environment around you, how you make the place better for others to live. I have learnt so much from him, tackle things how to deal office, and balance between life is very important otherwise it will ruin everything. It is said correct, "The importance of something is only till you get it and how you lose them after losing you understand how much important it was" but actually losing is not the reason it's the guilt that why you lost it and how it was taken away from you.

The character of your life is not what you decide they will stay as your wishes sometime, they just come and teaches you many things, it what we should learn and accept it but honestly accepting is just like someone had shot you on your head you still got 10 minutes to rewind your old memories.

CHAPTER 4

I just landed texted to Saurav, "Please reach near 6 PM at home"."Come to Hangover bro, "he replied. I asked; "Where it is?". He replied, "I am sending location you come there."I told ok I'm coming from airport I'll be reaching till 6pm approx... It's a rush our Bangalore being Bangalore too traffic I boarded the bus from Terminal 1 to KFC Indiranagar so I was chilled that I don't have to change anything its direct bus to my route.

Saurav called me and told that I am on way, Reaching in just 15 mins I hope you are on way. Actually I was late to be honest I just reached Indiranagar my flat around 5:40PM, I was too sweaty and tired and so I wanted to freshen up so, I just took bath in few minutes so I came out, my phone was ringing like anything it was 6 mixed calls with text written "Kaha Ho, come fast I'm at Hangover". I know I'm little bit late, I was meeting him for the first time in real, but we were friends from college as my whole college life went in Covid so online talks only, meeting him in real was difficult, knowing for more than 4 years.

Saurav and I was friend due to Mayank and his mutual friends. For the first time I saw him, it was just casually we hugged, and off course he was little bit angry as was really on time. We went inside Hangover; I was in black shorts with blue floral prints off shoulder tops. Saurav was wearing a white T-shirt with a blue jean, his hair was wavy, soft smooth with a white pair of sneakers and also having this in my mind that okay let's see him..." ab aur Kya hi bacha Hai ", The weather was very good little bit breezy air, and we sat on the table which was just next to many plants it was really giving a cozy vibe with little bit of dimmed light as he was my college friend so he mostly spoke about his friend circle about their Groups what they do in their college times what naughtiness they did in their college time. He told me everything, every single detail about his friends with whom he is staying and how much he loved them and how much he enjoy their company and he talks about Kshitij that he is so busy that he could not meet him before leaving to Los Angeles so he is little bit upset with him. Saurav work's for a software company named Accenture, and I had just started to write book, before I was working as an latest joinee in a research firm as I had just completed my internship program and all ; but I don't know what took so much time we talked till 9PM, it was huge year talks that every man would never wish to forget those Hostel days of his life. The manager came and wished me good evening with a glass of mango beer and chilli chicken it was all his favourite dishes. Saurav told, "Its late Esha, I'll drop you home". As it was late, he came and dropped me, we both were little bit drunk. He asked me a glass of water, I went to fridge, and gave him, he was little bit tired as he went from office, so was I. He told me he wanted to leave; I told its okay I am coming to drop you till gate. Saurav and I had a very warmth and balanced relationship, I always respected him but never saw him in a passionate way, as I know they work together. Last night I was very much upset, my mind was totally fucked up. Saurav was just leaving and told nothing he just kissed me, I saw he drank too much while having dinner, I wanted to stop him, but I have not kissed someone for many days, I couldn't resist, at first, I resisted thought it was a mistake, but I wanted him to kiss me back. Yes! I kissed him back, I don't know what was in my mind but couldn't resist him back, he was totally a good kisser though Saurav was a pro I know him since college, he was very charming and handsome just having a vibe full of attraction but never knew he could like me, for me it was a totally shock. He suddenly stopped himself as he realised that it's a mistake and he wanted to go back."You should leave right now, Yes| for sure you should go Saurav".

Sauravwas in the peak of his feelings, it was his emotions which was not at all in control that time, he did not want to leave, he wanted to kiss me, he was not sure what he wanted to do."Esha, I want us right now, I wanted you that's all nothing more than this right now, ", He was on the urge of getting me and I was just thinking he is a great guy but I was really confused what should I do now ?. It's not that he was forcing me, I guess we both wanted this due to our personal reasons, I was really upset because of my separation and he wanted to kiss someone as he had no physical intimacy since long back, he did not kissed anyone since so many days, so that night he couldn't stop himself. He was not able to control, at first I was not willing to kiss him, but I don't know when his hand touched me from back. I wanted someone to love me and really hug me back I just wanted someone to accept me that moment, I was really in emotions filled with suicidal thoughts, I was just thinking that I am very lonely and nobody accepts me the way I am but at that moment when Saurav hugged me I just felt as if I am belonged here. Saurav was very calm and understanding, I have not seen such a gentlemen, he really knows how to behave, how to care a women, I just don't know but he was really very comfortable man, he makes the environment calm and just made me feel very free from all thoughts, I was never having any nervousness with him, it was very just smooth nothing like any shyness nothing it was just real and transparent, everything what we know about each other is just very accepting. I don't know what time exactly it was but it was around 11 PM, he asked me, "Do you want this? I don't want to force you but truly I want you now and I am not thinking about anything more, it's between us and I want this right at this moment."I could think much but I wanted him to love me. I replied, "Yes, I don't know anything right now, but I want you to make me feel loved."Saurav kissed me, at first, he touched my hair, I felt ashamed, I could never feel so intensified and protected, I knew he won't leave me alone when I needed him the most. So, when he started to kiss me on my head at first, I felt so belonged; then face, ears and my necks my shoulder, I could not stop him, I guess he was the most romantic kisser one could ever have ;

he opened his shirt, for the first time I saw him like that, I don't want what to react, but looking him this way like that was very romantic plus full of lust.

Saurav knew how to impress girls through his kisses, hugs everything, he had done Ph. D. in all those things, while he was kissing me he touched my breast, I could not resist, I wanted him to suck me. The only thing that I wanted, was him to love me that's all nothing more than he loving me because I trusted him a lot, it was always more of a form of warmth in hiss hugs."Esha do you have condom", I told, "No".

For some time there was no voice I guess it was just so relaxing, I was going through a lot of tension and he just released all my stress and tension, obviously his charming nature made everything just a pleasant night.

"What you want from me Esha? Really Why are you so tensed just forget things can you just free yourself from everything right now. Baby try to relax yourself at this moment, right now it's only us so just look at me, I am here right with you, forget everything about past, I want you to live at this moment."

"I don't know I just want you to be with me that's all" (I hugged him and told him).

When Saurav kissed me on my breast, damn it was something the most killer time for any girl, I just wanted him to suck my whole body, I was just into him, nothing matters to me that time ...he went down, pulled off my legs start kissing my thighs, then he opened my shorts, ...he did not knew but actually it was my first time...I Never had sex with anyone before, ... It was something I really wished Mayank would do this for me, but that night I could not stop it, I just wanted Saurav to kiss me from top to bottom and every bit of me.

Suddenly Abhijeet called, Saurav was not picking his calls from evening he called two times, we did not saw it was around 2 AM in the morning, Abhijeet called and asked "Bro are you coming back or not?" Its me who did not wanted him to leave, I wanted him to be with me just stay near by my side. I know Saurav had to go to office early morning and I have to go to for my writing check-ups but still I wanted to be in his arms for whole night. Sometime I becomes a possessive one, a guy who is really tall, fair skinned, little bit of beard and that sexy eyes with specs and I am on his chest what a perfect moment. Its not about sex, I just loved to be in his chest and doing hickey on it and touching his hair, I see him like a perfect boy, I see his warmth vibe, I feel safe in his arms, I loved his passion to work but when he comes home, I just want to love him.

"Abhijeet I'll come tomorrow after work, I'll see you directly at Dinner tomorrow, today I won't be coming back, I'll see you tomorrow for sure."

Abhijeet really cared for him since college they are really very close so he just wanted to know and check, he is fine, so it was really very thoughtful of him, I really like the bonding what Sauravhad with his friends, I just admire their friendship like anything.

I don't know, why I kissed him but it was all of a sudden, somethings just happened it was never planned, nor Saurav did not me. I knew him for years but today I just wanted him, I did not thought about anyone, I just wanted my friend to be with me, whom I trusted a lot that he won't go leaving me alone. I knew Saurav won't hurt, when he touched my stomach, he asked me, "I am not hurting you na?". I liked the coziness and comfort what he gave to me, suddenly I forgotten all my stress.

I was kissing him, he touched me, I just put off the room lights, I don't saw anything but I could feel that his body was hot, when I touched his chest I could feel his heart was breathing very fast and he was also very happy at that moment, I could sense it that he was living at that moment. I don't know why I wanted him to be with me, I loved the way he just allowed me to be with him. I always wanted to love or make love with someone who wanted me to love him as my last relation looks as if I forcibly loved him and he was not that much interested what I wanted from him. Girls can relate who want to be with them or not it's the six sense. It's weird I was feeling very attached to him, but he was not.

CHAPTER 5

My head was in his chest, I wanted to have sex with him, but we just talked, it's strange, he touched me, his hand was in my chest, but I did not feel bad. I could feel it, it was intense, as if this was going to be. I was feeling tired, I wanted to rest in his arm, the whole night went off. We both slept over each other, it's the sun rays which came through my glass window, which opened my eyes, I saw him sleeping, at least I was seeing him first, I always wanted to be the first one, who he should see while waking up. Oh, shit it was 8am early morning I have to go and attend the meeting, reaching till 10 am, I don't want to wake up and leave him and go for work. I did not wanted to leave but its life, I just kissed in his forehead its Friday morning."Good Morning, I am going to work, you wake up have some tea I have kept for you I'll be seeing you at evening, I have back to back meetings order something for lunch and please do work from home, take rest you look tired, Okay". He was still sleeping "Okay I'll text you later, Bye have Good Day baby.."

I locked the door and went without making much noise so that he won't woke up(just very little bit of noise I made no much louder sound), I knew he was really sleepy and tired. I drove till metro station, took train from Indiranagar to Cubbon Park metro station, I had to attend the meeting on Brigade road, I could not be late, it was an important for my project, it was meeting with the Book leaf publication explaining about the process of my chapters and how it's going to be ? I could not be late, it was the agreement one, all paper work was on the process, I just had to sign the contract. I reached there at 10, the office was located at **Prestige Tower** Bangalore, 99/100, Residency Rd, Shanthala Nagar, Ashok Nagar, Bengaluru, Karnataka 560025. I was tired as I had to walk little bit from metro station but it was okay. My mood was little bit happy, though I should be upset due to my bad times, but I don't know I was feeling relaxed, I just was just smiling like anything, my glow can be seen I was just very fresh and my mind was all just very empty as if my all stress was just vanished, and I was not angry at all. I rush to lift, my meeting was at the tenth floor it's a co- working space, I was working with

Book leaf publication, it's a Noida based company so we took a co- working space in Prestige so that work meetings could be very organised and professional meetings would perform good. I totally believe work should be done on work environment, the seriousness of work, the creativity and agenda of the meetings, hiring every professional field require an office in which everyone give their best in the work. We have decorated the office with a grey look the whole floor is grey tiles, and the colour of the room is all grey but the lights are all LED lights so that the office is always bright and people would have a lighted environment, all chairs are white and there is a huge long length glass conference table in which everyone comes and discuss the agendas and problems regarding creativity, marketing strategies, sales and financial issues. My meeting was held to be in a conference hall, there is a huge long length glass table at the centre but there is one side full glass panels and the other side is a pure green wall decorated with natural twigs and plants so that work environment is filled with positivity. Glass panels are there so that the workspace is filled with natural sunlight making it as a blessing to work.

I had divided the office into one side conference hall and the other side, desks for all other working employees and there is small cafeteria, with table tennis area for refreshment zone. So we all sit and discuss everything together at conference hall, I believe in working with everyone as I think it should be always an open door policy in office so that everyone seems to be belonged there and there happiness and satisfaction is there in the workspace. All people should be allowed to speak and tell their grievances Infront of everyone so that office transparency is maintained and we all work together, for the betterment of the individual goals and as a whole for the company ;

The Editor and chief was going to come and talk with me and my team for the process of launching the book and the marketing strategies and launching date and how the media response is going on for the book launch. She arrived at 10:45 am, she told us to come and start meeting at 11 am. We all were at conference hall, it was me who had to lead about the ongoing process and the chapters which was completed, how the progress about the characters, and how much I had written and when it could be just completed, then the marketing team was going to take over then. At sharp 11 am, I started to talk in front of everyone at first, I was little bit nervous whenever you start speaking there is a sense of nervousness same goes with me. I started to explain from the screen that I gave a little bit of twist on the book, at first I thought there would be two protagonist on the story it would be dealing with not more than two protagonist but I changed the whole idea of two and now the main characters are not just two it is four and the crime and mystery revolves around these four characters. The main characters were Ritvik and Tia first but now I am adding Misha and Yash on the lead it's the teamwork who killed and removed all the evidences of crime. The story was about four college students who went to Pondicherry, the whole crime scenes took place there and the crime is not just about killing and hiding the crime scenes but its all about the audience would try to find the killer but, its not so easy to guess, Who's the killer ? I am making sure these four is not the killer. Then who is the killer? Its someone who is still missing in the crime scene or no body is introduced to the main killer.

I have wrote till 8 chapters and till there the killer is not yet came forward, everyone is trying to find the killer, the police and the audience itself and I am making sure the climax will be going to be a hit. I'll try to put more mystery on it. I want you all to read it and I 'll do it by the end of 15 days. I have showed the manuscript of all these 8 Chapters with the publishing house.

Mrs. Kate, "I like the idea of suspense and lets see how, much interesting you can make, you know Esha, its not easy to came a new twist on the last minute and putting a new character all together who will be responsible for all the deaths. I hope you have researched a lot and really have work done for the upcoming projects, you know na it has to be a hit, we can't take risk at all, we have put all our efforts in this project, we all want this project to be all good. I hope you have done research on it, Please do well and work with the team not against ",

"Yes mam I'll put my hard work and I will not let you down and my whole team is working with me. Just give me these days I'll put in a lot of hard work, and I will end it on time". Everybody liked it and accepted the idea, and I got little bit of appreciation and also deadline notice means over all it was a good one. Then my marketing team took over it and discussed a lot of changes and it strategies in a very unique manner that it should be available on social media but in a mysterious way. My whole meeting with all departments were till 2:30 pm, got little bit busy just saw the clock and thought its late. We had lunch break, everybody went for lunch so I called Saurav, why there is a caller tune in his call a senti one(tum kanha the yanha ...jane kabhi ye zamein ...) "Hi, have you eaten lunch ?" He replied, "Hi No Esha just was with my client call. How was your meeting? When you will be back?"

"I Knew that's why I ordered food for you, go and collect it, it's on way. I 'll be back by 5 we'll have coffee together by that time you complete your client calls."

I had lunch and started to write again, I knew I have to be a good one. My story was about to complete I had written everything that how four friends went to Pondicherry and they stayed in a hotel and there was a crime which took place. A mother was arrested to kill his own son but actually these four friends saw who did it, it was a mystery thrill combo, lets see who is the killer?

CHAPTER 6

I worked till 4:45 pm, I really want to be back home fast I just wanted to be in his arms. I punched at 5 pm, I know I was little bit early, but I really want to be back soon. I took metro to Indiranagar, I called him, "Where are you? Come to 100 FEET, we'll have tea at Shri Udupi Park".

"OK I'll be there in 20 minutes Esha". I took Uber and went to tea shop, I was little bit early, I waited for him. As usual he was late, I am sitting in the second next table, having a cup of tea, it's about to reach at 6pm."Where are you Saurav? I reached baby come fast na I am waiting for you." "I reached Esha let me come inside" (told in phone call)

"I am wearing a black top and black relaxed fit jeans and sitting in second table come in Saurav fast". For instance I was shocked, he was in black shirt with grey jeans as he was in work calls that's why he was looking very formal and sophisticated just like a gentleman, at first I laughed at his face.

I never saw him like that "What happened" he asked.

"Nothing you just look to formal, you know na it's a date not an interview Sir" I laughed. He blushed and told "Yes Yes stop laughing like this on me", he sat down but I could not stop my laughs, he was really looking cute but it was funny seeing him so formal, because I never saw him in the formals before.

"So how was your day Esha ? Is it a good one or a bad one?"

"My early morning was a fab, I guess. I saw a cute face who was in a deep sleep; I saw a baby at my bed who could not opened his eyes at early morning. He was so in a romantic mood of not leaving me also and not willing to let me go out for work. It's a cozy morning before work but going was also important. But altogether my meetings were good, but I have to pace my work little bit more. It was a good day all thanks to you".

He smiled, "off course". He ordered a cup of coffee, he is not a tea lover, typical of guy like him. We chatted about many things like he had a dog when he was in hostel everyone gave him food, that doggy comes in class with him to attend his lectures, everyone accepted this in class, so he was willing to buy a dog.

I refused, "Please first take care of yourself baby then try to be parent of a puppy, you and all guys who lives with you are also gone case. You all are whole day out for work, please bear with that puppy, it will require parenting when it is very small."

"Arey toh you come home na and take care of these puppies sometime and also hug me daily and off course (gently he smiled and in a very little voice) kiss also baby (he told its public babe little soft na)"."Ya Ya as if your whole family loves me a lot" in a sarcastic manner I said."Come na Esha you know I have to go home today, Abhijeet called me and told, its Varu's birthday bro, today you have to be with us" I could not deny them.

"Come baby, you will see everyone, you don't meet with them I know but come na meet everyone today, I want you to be with me in the party, I want you to interact and get close to my friends".

"SauravI know they won't like it and you know na its Varu's birthday. Please go and enjoy with them and you know na I have to go to Ranchi for some days so, I have to pack my luggage and complete my work also. You also know I have a night flight tomorrow so I can't party na."

"I wish you come with me Esha, I want Rudy to meet you and I want you to meet everyone." "I know babe but it's not the right time, we should take some more time. Let us first know each other more than we know us right now, definitely then, I shall talk and meet with all your friends surely."

"What Babydoll you want me to leave, wow what a perfect bye and you are leaving tomorrow night. Don't you think it's not right, you leaving so early for 10 days." "I know but you also know na I have some work in Ranchi so I have to visit home for some days I have to meet my grandmother and mom n dad because it's my younger sister birthday on 10th May so, I have to visit Babe, I'll come back soon and you will be with me, after then you will be with me in a cage for months." "I want to be with you Esha, yesterday we were together, and now you are going for so many days why ?"

"It's not like that Saurav my tickets was done long back my brother will also come there, so there is a kind of get together, I have to attend she is small and you know we all want to surprise her, she is my cute little princes so, I have to be with her and as I am the elder one I should be there, it will make Suku very happy so Please try to understand baby. Don't think it's too much days, just think like that I will be back soon think little like that na, then you will not feel so bad babe." "But Esha I have started to miss you from now only, babe so many days you will be out. Okay I will come at night after party, please now don't argue na I just want some time with you."

"Okay Saurav let's go home now, you have to go to party".

We return back to my house in 7th cross, Eshwara layout, he had to get ready and go to party, suddenly he was feeling very hot, he was like baby, "I want to stay in hotel today I don't want to attend party I am feeling very hot" that time Bangalore heat was too much, he genuinely wanted to rest, last night also, he was not sleeping so, I accepted that he really wanted to sleep. He was in bed, booking room for that night so that we can chill and rest in AC, I was busy in work so did not got time to buy AC and all and I thought when I will return I 'll check and buy AC. Saurav booked a hotel Park Prime, let's go rest and will come next day he told "Babe lets go na will rest, it's in Indiranagar only C'mon get ready we are going for sure, we really need time for us and you are also going, Come I am booking uber lets go". I was just like a lazy girl who stays at home, pink shots and black crop top, I told "baby let me take shirt on it, you watch movie, I will take some rest"."Esha come fast baby, why you take so much time?" "Saurav let me wash my face at least, I am looking so dull, Baby why are you shouting at me, hold my purse and lock the gate." "Really Esha I need to hold your purse (he looked at me in a sarcastic manner)." "Off course babydoll, put yourself used to this from now onwards forever, after some days you will be used to this" (I smiled in front of him when he was really very angry and pissed off from me).

After 20 mins we reached the hotel Park Prime near Trinity metro station, Saurav did the check in and we got room number 1501, it was a double bed with AC, his first preference, it was around 8pm when we reached there, I was in bed resting for some minutes, he closed the lights, he was watching match in his laptop with his earphones, I was in deep sleep. He woke me up very gently and told, "Babe dinner is there I have ordered I am going to collect it please lock from inside"."Okay come fast please". He brought some burgers and chicken wings his favourite and told me to eat and rest. He was busy watching his match it was RCB and Chennai IPL match he was really excited for that match so I could sense he will be in full mood for cheering Kohli and his team. I went to deep sleep, it was all dark night and chill as AC was on 16 DEGREES, Saurav always wanted cool, so it was fine for me too. My called mom and asked "Have you eaten beta?, all good? Okay Good night I'll see you tomorrow, send me the tickets so that I can pick you up."

"Okay mom good night, I'll send you the tickets you don't worry bye good night".

Saurav was busy watching the match, the match was on a high pace, everyone was excited as it was like RCB was just winning I guess Virat Kohli was sure that, his team had played fab, it was really interesting and excited match between them whole Bangalore was watching the match I could hear the boys and girls down near the pool celebrating the winning of the match, they were shouting "RCB What a match" I could see the wining vibe of everyone it was good that people are so excited, it was a historic match for everyone. Everybody was really happy, Saurav was really excited, he really woke me and said, "let's have a cup of tea"."Really right now babe? Have you seen the timing its 12 am at midnight. If you really want to go, then okay let's go down let's walk and have a cup of tea" (I was still in bed, I was lazy did not wanted to wake up and walk a little bit)."Okay I am making tea for us both and now you come to balcony at least baby please". He really heated the water and made a tea and told me come to balcony, I am waiting. He was shirtless, enjoying his cold cozy vibe, whatever he wanted, he was standing in the balcony on 15th floor I was just admiring him because I was going for some days. I was just seeing him; my eyes were not stopping, and I was just looking at him while he was looking outside the balcony. I went to him and hug him from back and said "Baby why are you so cute, you look damn hot, I wish to kiss you now, the night is so cozy full moon and you being here, it's just you and me, I always wanted this that when I met someone who really loves me, I wanted that I'll be with him in this peaceful night, and I just want to admire you". He was not blushing at all, but he laughed.

"Really babe you are laughing I' am flirting with you and you are laughing haw.. baby you destroyed our sweet moment, I am really in a romantic mood and you being you destroyer of the whole romance".

"No babe first have your cup of tea, it's going to be cold, take it". I was drinking tea and thinking, 'I guess I have done something good in my life that I could be with him right now, this moment was just fab, I am with you, why you did not come in my life before, I wished you came in my life before sometime but still I don't want you to lose you anymore. I have not spent many times with you, but I just don't know why right now one think I just want that you be with me every minute from now.

"Esha I don't think about romance I just do it, you will get to know more closer now". Saurav always believe in living in the present moment, I really liked that thing about him that he always gives himself first preference in his own life, I really admire him, it's not lust or anything I just felt attached to him. I really don't know what he really think, but I was really getting attached to him, though I met him for some days I was just feeling that this is the guy I really wanted to be with. He was standing in the balcony and having cup of tea, faced towards the moon, seeing the moon, skies, stars just having his me time, and what I was doing is just admiring him, how it is possible that I am feeling so attached to him, I am not able to think that he can go I am just really want him fully, I don't want to wait, I am not able to have patience, my last relation I was really very patient but this time I want to be with him, I don't know why it happens when you want to say these things to him, but I waited though, he deserves more than this. I just want to give him as much love as he never thought of this much love can someone give him.

I always wanted someone to love me more but when he was there, its not anymore that I want love, its just that I want to give him more love, he always don't say many things but I know he is thinking too much, but I know men they are not able to speak that much. I went to him and kissed, he was blushing, at first he was shock, "What happened babe, you look little bit tensed?"

"Yes I don't want to loose you now, please, (I was having little tears in my eyes)I just don't want anyone to separate us, please, I hope we are always together please."He hugged, "Yes babe, its us okay, don't worry I'll not leave that's for sure". His hand was in my hair, he kissed in my head, "No one will come in between us, I'll be there with you always from now I promise that no matter anything you will find me with you standing right beside you."

We were close to each other, it was a cosy moment, I was in his arms, I just felt warmth, happy protected and what more I can get from this life, whenever he is with me I said, "Baby Please kiss me right now." "Esha you are going tomorrow you should rest little bit please babe not now"."No Saurav please kiss me, please don't think."He kept his hand on my mouth and kissed at my right side of my neck. He touched me, but something was in his mind, what I will think as he told me come lets go to hotel, so I might not judge him that he just see me for sex and all. I could sense it,

"Baby I am not judging you, but I want us."He kept his hands on my eyes,

"Don't open it, he took me to room, kissed me on my neck, I could smell Saurav's body odour, it was very manly, I could feel his presence, he hugged me so tightly from back, I could feel his face on my hair, I was calm but I had a sensitive feeling and he wanted to show that I am there with you. He made me sit in bed and told "please wait for some minutes don't open your eyes". I thought what he was doing, I could smell he was doing something with candles."Open your eyes baby" I saw he had decorated the whole room with the candles and in the floor it was all red rose petals. The whole room he had decorated with candles and the smell of fresh rose petals, he had put the curtains all covered over the balcony, at work table suddenly I could see a bunch of flowers on it and there was so many candles the cozy environment made me so special, I was shocked. He also decorated the bathroom tub with, rose petals and scented candles, I was feeling really special no one did this more me till now. He hugged me and kissed me, "Come with me". He carries me over his shoulder and took me to the bathroom, it's just having a glass wall, the room can be seen from bathroom, it was very transparent. He put me down on the floor, while I was standing, he kissed me in my shoulder, he pulled off my black, tan top so gently, he admires me, sees me. I asked him, "What you want?". He answered, "YOU". I smiled, I blushed,

I was just seeing him, he was so cute, I loved the way how caring he is. He is really handsome if I really notice him sometimes, I think love is not something a fire or a burning desire but it just gives your face a shine that comes naturally, you can't stop laughing, the excitement of new love and friendship, the new bonding and attachment, more peace and calmness and all together its just makes you feel special that someone is as attached to you as you are attached to him. Saurav's chest was so smooth and clean, his beard I love him more when he is in beard, I had buried all my emotions in the ground long back but when I see him I just think I can blossom once again. I like him in this way, when he is so romantic, intense and so passionate for me, I always wanted a guy who admires me and respect me like he does."Are you comfortable with me Esha?" "Yes Saurav why are you asking me this, I have not met you many times I know, but I feel very comfortable with you naturally, it's something that I feel very satisfied with you, being with you makes me whole and integrated and the smile on my face is all because of you".

I went near him, I looked in his eyes, I touched his specs removed it, with specs he looks very workaholic, always busy at work but I only wanted him, just mine.

I closed my eyes and kissed him so passionately whenever, I see him with his friends or colleagues trust me, I just smiled and think he is mine and to be honest just get lost everybody and leave us alone here. Whenever I see any of his friend comes and greets him, hug and wish him, I just feel so jealous of every girl who works with him, I don't know why but I always wished, I met him early before anyone else came in my life. But now when he is just in front of me, I hugged him, he is so tall really, I feel like a small girl in front of him. Saurav looked at me with full attraction; started to kiss me, he opened my red bra hook, at first he could not open it and laughed told, "Shit not again baby, I like to open your clothes and this hook why it's so strong, (I smiled at him) Don't laugh now you are going to be mine for sure. I was shy when he was looking at me like this, [Saurav] "Alone at last (shudders), I am with you, that's good (sighs), come inside water, he gave me his hand, helped me to get inside warm water[clear throats]. I gasps Ow, ow [laughs]my half body was inside hot and warm water, my body could feel the density of water, the volume was little bit up, but I was able to breathe properly, from one hand he put rose petals on me and said, "I want to love you like this daily babe, just give me one chance

Please, I'll sort of everything, and we will live happily like this, I want to be with you babe always, whenever I am not with you, I think when will work get over and I will be back with you."The darkness of bathroom was scaring me, he gave his hand, and said, "You do kind of like it, though, note it I am all yours from now and everyday". I closed my eyes he took both my hand, in his hands and kissed me on my neck, gently he went down, suck my breasts, he was inside water, "Are you okay babe?" "Trust me, I am fine just don't think anything and don't speak too much babe, how much you speak Esha, shut up otherwise I have to kiss you so much that you can't speak anything, only this can close your mouth I guess".

He sucked my breasts, from one hand he was pressing my boobs (it was so pleasurable, he knew I was more likely to have an orgasm right now)."Suck my boobs baby, please don't stop, it's all yours, I want you to fuck me

Hard" [Esha].

I always wanted someone to love me like this, he was kissing me, pressing my boobs, sucking it, kissing it, simply sucking or licking my nipples. The wet suction noise of sucking on my boobs, and his tongue licking my nipple area, made me feel into his world with so much romance and pleasure."Keep doing that, it feels so good baby". He kissed my stomach, went down, kissed on my thighs, he puts his finger on my vagina, "Saurav now you have two options left, either you fuck me hard, or you leave right now".

"Wait a minute, let me bring condom, help me with this, he told last time his ex-helped him so", "Baby it's my first time." "Really Esha not with Mayank also, or anybody else". [Esha] "Baby I was in a relationship, so thought I will do it in a correct time, and it never came"."Okay we can do it, but it might be difficult little bit because first time it pains little bit. If you don't wish it's okay no pressure baby, I am asking, we will do it only when you want, please don't take any pressure on yourself babe." "I don't know I am sure or not, but I want to love you now". Saurav was always understanding, this is what I liked about him, his care towards me, the way he used to take care about me, the first preference he gives me and my feelings.

"I am sorry babe, I should have told you about this, I know you might be offended that you did so much, and I am not so ready for that"."No, I am not babe, I love you the way you are, Esha but we will experiment today don't worry, you just trust me, babe be relax its me".

He returns back inside the water, kissed me on my lips, shoulders, neck, he went down kissed me on my stomach, he puts his finger in my vagina, trying to turn me on, he was on full mood that time.

"I love it when you hit that spot" (I was getting wet).

At first, I was not sure, "Baby I am little bit scared"."Trust me, I am here", he first to tried to put his penis inside my vagina at first it pained me little bit, I screamed; little bit of bleeding, I knew that I will get pain but I was sure, he is with me, at first my body was not loose, it was rigid, it's my first time so it was normal to be like that. I looked at him, I was loving the way he was so excited for sex but for me he was so comfortable and making me so loved, I appreciated him. He is the only person I met with whom I am really open to, I don't have to think anything before speaking to him. l am really being open and honest towards him; with him I am seen heard and most important he understands me, living and sleeping with a man does not mean we are close it's the warmth which makes you feel closer, attached and loved. We had sex, he did this for so many seconds, I was not wanting him to stop, he repeated this motion till we both got comfortable with each other's body.

"Are you fine, I hope I have not hurt you Esha? He kissed me on my forehead,

"I just want you to be happy baby, I just can't hurt you, never ever I can hurt, I just want to protect you forever, Esha"."Babe please don't speak, I want to be with you right now, I don't want to think anything just please it's us, don't think please". I kissed him, "I know many things had happened, but this is meant to be, why it is there we can't be just us, why there is so many of us included. I like you; I know saying this too early, but I can't keep it with me, I never thought it's going to be but it's the truth of my life, I don't know what was in my past was true or this, but this definitely I always wished for. I am really attached to you, I know there is nothing to hide and everything can be said to you, I know you are my best buddy but you are just more than this, I am emotionally dependent on you, you come first in my life, you are great partner and I am really thankful that you came in my life".

Saurav took me out of water, cleaned me with towel with lots of care, I could see his intense eyes with love and care for me, he gently carried me in his shoulders and took me to bed, "Whole night I'll kiss you, love you, I won't let you think anything else than us". He opened the hotel room fridge, took out the chocolate syrup, took one spoon and made me eat it, "Esha, this sweet is for us, it's not two, from today we are one and forever"."Please lie down and close your eyes, he tied my hands together and told me to just be relaxed and trust him; he puts all the chocolate syrup on me, I could feel the whole chocolate was flowing from the top of my head, slowly coming down to my stomach, Saurav kissed every part of my body where the chocolate syrup was flowing; I could feel his tongue kissing my boobs, he wanted to love me whole night, he did love bites everywhere the chocolate syrup was going in my body, I kissed him, in his chest, I was not thinking anything at this moment, just one thing that it's us, I was feeling guilty about being so selfish but in case of Saurav, nothing comes in my mind accept him. We both wanted to make love, I touched his hair, "Please don't cut your hair, I like it, many times we fight but that night it was only about love and love, some people might think its lust but there is a fine line between lust and love i. e. you just want to see the other person happy with or without you, but its all about him being the first one in your life, his freedom all about you care. Actually true love is very patient, kind, you are not jealous, you are not forcing, you are not rude, its never demanding, its not a situation of win or loose it's just there. Love will never gave upon you, its always hopeful, you will smile on your own, it's the reason for you to have faith in God and the most important love will give you respect, you both will recognise each other's opinion and both will value each other. For me, he was all about miracle, who came in my life and made me feeling of a soulmate in just so shortest period of time.

The whole night, we kissed and had sex, it was about 5 am early morning, he asked me for a cigarette, "Babe I don't have it, you know na that I don't smoke so why would I keep it Saurav", he searched for it, he could not find it, "Babe I am really tired, I want to take rest little bit, you also sleep na". I took his arm, kissed him on his cheeks, "Good night, sleep now, we have to wake up also". I slept on his arm, at first, I saw him, he was awake, he is having the habit of sleeping late, as he works at night, so he was going to sleep on his timings. I slept in a deep sleep, because of chilled weather and off course him, and the cozy morning. I love to sleep in early morning, I feel it's the best sleep when its little bit cool, sun is going to come but all together I love the early morning vibes. Saurav kissed on my lips and woke me up "Good morning baby, its time we have to get ready and leave for airport. I have made tea for you common go freshen up, then we will go down and have breakfast at restaurant they had called us for breakfast, its already 9 am we have to be there before 10:30, I am going to take shower, you wake up till then, "Do you want me to come Saurav, with you, do you need any help from me". He smiled little bit, "Baby you will never stop flirting with me na, not now, let me get ready babe, I know you will take time, so let me get ready first". While he was taking shower, I made the bed, while having cup of tea, I don't like to leave hotels so messed up and dirty, I try to keep it as it is in my room, I packed up my charger and winded up my stuffs in my bag. I was having a cup of tea, my mom called "Good morning Kuhu, we are going to work, send me the tickets, at night we will be surely there to pick you up"."Okay mom, I will be sending it and I'll leave airport on time, okay call you back later."He was taking shower, I was wishing to go and see him, I know I am too much into him these days but for him, its never the end, he is just really cute.

He came out of the shower, "Where is my shirt baby, I Know you have kept it". "I'll not give you back, I like seeing you like this, my baby Saurav, who is the master of the art", he started to laugh, common go fast have shower early and come fast baby we are getting late. I went to bathroom, got freshen up in 20 mins, I came out, and saw he was waiting in bed for me, seeing his phone, "are you done babe ?"."Saurav Yes| where is my pant yaar give it na its in my bag that white one, he gave me and I finally got ready, we both always dressed as a couple, I wore the black T-shirt with light shade beige pant and he was wearing, a grey shirt with dark blue jeans, I laughed "What baby you are looking so damn hot, don't wear shirt in front of me, I will be opening the buttons right now, "Enough babe lets go down its going to be 10:15, come on, "he was angry and I was making him laugh, we both stood in front of mirror, he kissed me "Good morning, baby I hope you slept peacefully, let's go, keep things here just take the keys of the room"."Yes go and press the lift babe, now you are getting late", he gave me silent look, which I understood that he is angry for being late. We both went down at the restaurant, there was no body accept we both, the hotel staffs asked "What you like to have Mam?"."Great ask only mam, I need one cup of coffee", Saurav asked in a sarcastic manner, as he annoyed me being late, he was getting for late work."Baby sorry, what should I get for you, tell me na Saurav, ", "Get me some sandwiches and you eat fast, we have to leave also baby". I ate some dosa and he had his coffee and he went to reception, did all the formalities and we went back to room. He was in bed waiting for me to pack everything, I asked "Baby drink some water take bottle, why are you so angry"."No I don't want it now, where you last kept the bottle baby". For a second, I got confused, where I kept last, I went near him, and kissed him in his forehead, he blushed. I can't stop admiring him, I was really getting into him, trying to control myself as I was leaving, I don't know he is so sweet, why."Babe have you done the check in, I cant stop looking at his face, he is just super cute, I went and kissed him, for me leaving him so difficult, I just can't."Lets go Esha, we have to go to home, then take your bag too". He dropped me at home, told me to pack some clothes and told he is coming from office he had one meeting so I had time of 1 hour, that was enough for me. I thought I will do something for him, he did such a beautiful night for me, he should get something in return, something special. We must leave for airport at 2pm so that I may reach airport till 4pm, my flight will depart at 6 :10pm sharp, so time was running too fast, and my brain is not working at all.

While I was preparing myself to leave suddenly, I got pain in chest little bit, I was over excited happy, and my life was going okay but one thing I always knew that my tachycardia is never gonna go. I did not informed Saurav about my chest pain thought I will go home and do my checkups why to give him tension. I was willing to do something, but I was genuinely not feeling well, I had forgotten my morning dose, I was so busy with him that my mind slipped.

He calls" Baby, are you ready? I am on way coming just be ready, as soon as I come, we will leave for airport." "Yes, Saurav you come I'm ready". He was reaching in few minutes, but still I could sense the pain, I panicked I was alone, and I was thinking I should go or not, it was really painful when your heart rate increases more than 100, the palpitations had started at pace, I was feeling very tired, I was sweating too much; I understood I will not get relief till I will vomit, the shortness of breath was scaring me at that time, but honestly I was not scared for my self but at that moment I was only scared about losing him and not able to live with him. But I always thought more about him, I don't want him to be stressed because of me rather I always want to be the reason of his happiness. Actually, I was having severe tachycardia problem since childhood did not wanted Saurav to be tensed up so I thought I will go to Ranchi, I can manage till then. I was going for a long leave so, I will do all the checkups there so, I wanted him to be just okay here. Saurav came at 2:15, I did not informed anything about my pains, he came and hugged me, his eyes was little bit watery but he will not show any kind of emotions to me, I know him, he always hides his stress but do everything for me without any expectations. He took my one small luggage and one handbag, and said, "Come back soon, Esha", kissed on my right side of neck and hugged me. I saw him, he was just trying to pretend that he is okay, he told, "Come to car, I am taking your bag, lock it properly, I am waiting at gate."The whole ride he was not saying anything, it was just the silence, I could only here the traffic of Bangalore, he did not started any music, we both were thinking something, me thinking about my health it is okay or not, he was also thinking about something that I can see on his face. While he was driving, I could sense he wanted to speak to me, but Saurav is not so vocal about his problems, he always try to solve by himself. We reached airport at around 4:15pm, I thought he will say something at least I love you, or baby don't just go be with me right now I need you, but he did not spoke anything. He took out my luggage from car, and saw me with deep intense look, said, "Come out Esha you are getting late, Come fast". I came out tears where in my eyes, I was pretending it was all okay, he gave me bags, he was standing in front of car taking the support of the bonnet, I was seeing him, his hair, beard which I love a lot, his specs eyes, him in grey shirt with blue jeans, and black shoes, I knew I was not going to see him for many days, I went near him, saw all around everybody was busy in their work and everyone was in a hurry so nobody was seeing, I kissed him in his neck, he was shocked, I hugged him, I was just smelling his body odour, I don't know when I was going to smell it again, I was just being at that moment, thinking nothing just being there."Esha go its time now, come soon, just come back soon, I will be waiting for you come to me soon"."Baby I can stop if you say, please tell me if anything is bothering you, please?" "No Esha please you are really getting late, call me after doing security check, I am waiting outside, you call me just go now baby its late, it's so full go now otherwise you will say you missed flight because of me". I took my luggage and hand back took out my pan card showed to the CISF officer at the gate of

Kempe Gowda International Airport Bengaluru and get inside the check in baggage counter, I saw there is a huge line, I was getting late, my line was really very long, I was just praying to God that please I should not miss it, it was going to be 5 soon, I just completed any how the luggage check in, this run was giving me anxiety, somehow I managed and went to security check, and the problem comes there, as it more time consuming, remove water from bag keep it in a small checking tray and take out every gadgets, in Bengaluru airport this is the most anxiety area as you have to run to the boarding gate but the security process really was taking too much time than other airports, I was getting late, my boarding was going to start from gate number 27 which was down stairs, after completing all my checks I was running towards the gate, Saurav called me, "Baby where are you, is it all okay ?"

"Baby wait okay I will call you back, I was just in a rush towards the boarding gate. Saurav was just outside airport having coffee so that if I missed the flight, he would be there for me, he is really an understanding one but I know he does not show much from outside.

I reached the boarding just on time, they were calling my name on final call, I somehow managed to board the plane, finally I called Saurav, "Baby I just boarded now that time I was running, I did not wanted to miss the flight so sorry",

"Haan bolo, Esha stop it, it's okay, now you should sleep in flight, whole night you did a lot of work baby, you must be tired enough, Take some rest, I am here in airport I'll be leaving after sometime, I started to miss you from now, see you soon okay, okay bye call me after landing bye baby, " "Okay I'll call you after reaching there, Please drive safe, okay". I also called mom, "Mom I boarded I'll be reaching around 7:50pm, please come and pick me up"."Yes, Beta we will be there". For 2 hours I went to deep sleep, I was really tired, just wanted to be relaxed, I knew Saurav will reach home safely, I thought about him, I was just thankful to God that he was in my life, whenever I am in flight, I try to be thankful and that is why I sleep so relaxed without any tension, I know I have a great supportive family, who loves me a lot. I landed after 2hrs and 15 minutes, it was about be 8pm, as soon as signal started, I called Saurav, "Where are you baby, I just landed and did you reached babe ?, order your dinner please babe".

"Okay Esha, I'll call you at night you go home first".

CHAPTER 7

I was excited to meet my mom, she is always very talkative, so much strict with me, as all the mothers are, but I was really very happy that I was going to see her after many days, my excitement was at its peak level. As soon as the announcement of the belt was going on from where I could get my bag, my mom texted, "We are at the exit gate as soon as you collect the bag, you come out fast we are waiting there". I replied, "Okay coming fast". After collecting the bag, I went out I saw my mom, she was just near the car, my father was at the driving seat, he told, "Come fast beta, otherwise police will come to remove us from parking come fast". As soon as I sat on car there was a kind of relief that I am at home, I opened the window of my car, saw outside I saw the airport runway and the trees with the wind blowing, I was so feeling calm that finally I reached without any health issues, for some minutes I just forgot that I was out for so many days, tears came to my eyes, it was of happiness. Whenever I comeback I just feel the air, something is different in Ranchi's wind, it will make you fall in love with the cool breezy vibes. My father drove the car till home, as soon as I reached home, Super started to shout and bark, he sensed it, that I'm home, I feel so homely and welcomed that this is it, my zone. My mom told, "Just go freshen up and then come to eat dinner okay"."Yes mom I'll be soon coming to kitchen". I went home texted, "Baby I'll call you after dinner okay, you please eat it"."Yes Esha, I am also going to eat okay". As soon as I enter the room I saw everything was at its place, it was all constant, it gave me the feeling of where I belonged, it made me feel wherever I will go for work, whenever I will come back everything will be the same, nothing will change, it gives me so comfortness that its my house, no wonder I am out but when I will come back everything will be same as you last saw it, everything is constant, it made me so happy from inside that yes it's my room it's just mine, in life everything is changing but when you come home and see everything is constant, it feels like a security and reliefness that no matter what my home will be mine.

In the process of my excitement, I had really forgot about someone who is really may be upset suddenly he is all alone at home (in Bangalore). For me, home is just peace as soon as you go, you sometime just forget things but that does not mean that the love for him is decreased. After dinner and talking with my parent's little bit they told me to talk to them the next day as I was tired, they told me to go to bed and take some peaceful sleep.

I tried calling Saurav, he must be tired after dinner he went to sleep. If he did not pick up my phone, I understood he was tired, so he slept.

But for me sleeping without him is an issue, I went to bed trying to sleep but at first I could not sleep, I was used to sleep in Saurav's chest, I love to play with Saurav before sleeping he always wanted to kiss me and me being me, I love to make his romantic mood into a comedy one. I was just thinking about him, that I hope he sleeps well I am concern about him always just want him to be calm and peace while resting without any tension, when I last saw him I knew he was stressed about work little bit but he was trying to hide with me but I could feel whatever tension he was going through so I wanted him to just be relaxed and I am always with him, though I'm far currently. For me Saurav is just not the one whom I admire but the one who is my buddy, my that friend that I know if everyone will leave me to but he will be with me standing. My bed is very cozy, Ranchi vibe is just different because the wind, which was coming inside through window, is so silence, peaceful, I always wish that I will call Saurav here so that he may feel it the calmness and the natural air which comes here. As it was my first night, I was not able to sleep, I just went to balcony so that I will have some fresh air and then I could sleep with peaceful mind. I saw the moon the balcony with fresh smell of flowers, the breezy wind which was blowing everything was there except him, I don't always think about him but at night in think about him, I pray to Krishna and Radha that whatever might happen the love between us should not fade. I will work very hard for achieving my goals but this I prayed to be constant forever the bond between us. No wonder my thought process is so bad if you have a partner like him then definitely you can't sleep,

I was looking at moon and praying that one day definitely, he will be standing with me having a cup of tea and I will be with him, it's my father's home, I really respected him and I wanted him to accept Saurav and also that my family is happy because of us and we stay together with the beauty of joy and happiness. I don't know that this person who came in my life all of a sudden but truly I don't want him to leave me. Whenever I feel week its him he makes me fight against problems, I knew him from college but I never thought that one day nothing else will matter to me accept him, I wish that he stays in my life.

Someday you meet someone so sudden that he becomes your life, love is so special you don't have any kind of blood relation you don't know how you are connected to him but his little bit smile on his face makes you feel so special. Last night I bought munch for him, he was happy that I did for him, he was a person who deserves love a lot, a caring person, a trustworthy friend, a man who understands the importance of job, who is serious in life who scolds me to work hard and write a good book, he teaches me the importance of opportunity and how we should respect the chance which is given to us, he makes me a strong women who should have the opinion, he always makes me be an independent women not only emotionally but he explains me the importance of women being financially independent. Boys like this is a real gem. It's not always we are always happy we are two different person but if we fight we should try to sort things, but sometime I am sorry for my behaviour because he tries to be cool but I know many times I shout at him in anger and that is not correct, neither a boy or a girl should shout at each other in anger times rather one should try to make the other person understand the behaviour and make her or his understand how things can be okay and how it should end in a peaceful note.

It is very important to have a person in life who guides you, who makes you see yourself at mirror, love is not giving gifts or telling other person to see me daily, rather love will make you free from everything it will give you wings to fly, just like you don't pluck flower when you love them rather you water them daily. One thing I love the most in him, he appreciated the similar things between us, but he respects the differences what we both have.

I went back to my room, closed the balcony doors thought that I should sleep as my body was too tired, soon after some minutes I went to sleep. I slept at around 2 am, it was just so peaceful vibes, so I was in deep sleep. My mother woke me up around 7 am, she told me, "Wake up Kuhu, get ready fast, we have to go to church on time, the mass is going to start at 9 am you should be on time, we should all go together, there is going to be a thanksgiving so get up Kuhu". I was at home my dad is just super cool, he keeps tea just near my bed and comes and hug me and say, "Good morning, beta go wake up now", my dad had really pampered me and my sister, he always wakes me up with tea, so I am used to this kind of environment so always wanted this cozy environment with Saurav too. My home is really peaceful because my father has a big role in it, I belonged to a matriarchal society, my dad gets super angry on some days but still, I always saw him trying to talk in a soft manner, he tries to control his anger. I woke up went to bathroom and started to brush my teeth, took bath went to kitchen, I saw my mother cooking puri and sabji for us, till that day I took everything for granted, but I saw my mother wakes up first, drink coffee for herself and works little bit, oh sorry I forgot to introduce, my mother is a working professional but she was on the process of doing Ph. D. so she has to work on her project, she was a women beyond compare, though I become an adult but she will treat me like a 10 year kid, I know it sounds kiddish but my mom always don't allow me to grow in front of her I am still that little baby girl. She scolded me, "Kuhu learn to cook something, its basic need, she gave me wheat and told me to make puri", I was like yes I can do it, but when I took it, I could feel it, mothers work hard daily but they don't utter a word that they are tired, my sister and I was used to eat mothers food daily my brother too but never understood why mothers food are super delicious it's because mothers really shower blessings through their food. The way what mothers show their love is by their behaviour, mothers never say I love you but the behaviour of them showed how much care they do for us. We mostly forgets the love for mom but no love is limited actually love should be unlimited, love should always spread and the hatred should be try to decrease. I saw my father coming to kitchen, my mother commented, "Kya sir breakfast is ready, Sir kiska baarat hai, aap itna saj dhaj ke aye ho, now eat breakfast I m going to get ready". After cooking for everyone my mother went to take bath, then I realised how phenomenal she is, she is a women a teacher and now she is a student how, warmly without stressed she manages home and work. I like the way, how she balances home and work both. When I was a kid I was always used to be upset and angry on my mother because she left me in my grandfather's place as she had to go to work and earn money, our financial condition was not so good enough that my mother could keep me with herself so she always comes on Saturday. I still remember though she did not have money with herself she used to live in Pakur district near small village, she works as a doctor there in government hospital in a small village near Bansloi river it was a beautiful small village where too much of snakes was there, I knew in my kid times I could see my mother only on Saturday and Sundays and regarding my father for months I could not see him, he was also working out I could see him only on my parent teacher meeting when I was going to new class. My mother use to come at Saturday evenings, she for surprising me used to keep one lays which was worth 10 Rupees and I remember one big coca cola which was worth 40 Rupees at that time in 2001 year, everything was big because she wanted me to have these chips and nuts for whole week so that I was not becoming upset, every women would do anything for making their child have a better future. She thought I did not knew about that she used to keep it in cupboard but I always knew it that my mom used to keep it so that I play hide and seek find them and be happy. My dad was also working in government area at rural area there was no telephone that time so he could not come so easily he used to work at rural place inside a small village too but not with my mother that's why he does not come frequently, his main aim was to work hard and earn money for our better future. I don't regret for my childhood days because my grandfather and mother both loved me so much that I never missed my mother and father too I could not see for many months I could see my father's only on New Year's Eve.

For many years I was upset with my parents that they never been with me on my childhood days but then now I realised that how much painful was that time for my parents. When I grew up from that day my parents started to stay with me after my grandfather died that was a bad time for us then, my father had to return back and started to find job here because no one was there with me, how much alone my grandmother could take care of a small girl. But those where days I always respect and cherish and now when my dad came with a cup of tea and taking breakfast near, I was lucky enough that I could see my dad now and he eats with me.

While we both were eating and gossiping about mom, my father complain me about his diabetes issue, that she is not taking care of herself, we thought to take class of my mom rather we got to know that our number will come fast. My little brother and sister with Super had done their breakfast so we were ready that only mom was left for breakfast, I always thought what

I can do for my mom but actually I cannot reach that level on first also, how can I reach her level in just some days, I know I am here only for some days. My mom came, my dad gave her the medicine for diabetes, I always admire the bond between my mom and dad; I always wanted my relationship to be like them. I just wished that my parents stay like this, it's not always a good times, they were with me on my bad times always standing beside me. I always misunderstood that my parents don't love me but it's all that my parents wanted me to be happy from inside and do something which is best for me. My family environment was so good, that I find myself lucky enough that it is okay, I loved my family for always supporting me, being with me and always being grateful to them, I just wish that someday I make my parents proud of who I am and who I really want to be. I wish to be a good human being and that my parents feel immense proud seeing me, they be happy and they respect me equally what I do to them.

CHAPTER 8

It was a beautiful sunny Sunday morning everyone was ready to go to GEL Church Main road Ranchi, where I used to go when I go to Ranchi, we were on car, and as every family scene car is a place of discussion, my father connects my phone with car and he is always interested to listen music he is like Esha play some music I want to hear it, my mother was always a talkative one but my dad was just the opposite, he is chill person, who loves to hear some music and drive car while he is driving, his main agenda is to distract himself of all tensions but wants everything to be little bit cool.

After reaching to church, we prayed their attended mass for almost 1 hour, I was lucky that I had a great Sunday, my mom wanted to make chicken curry for me so, she bought chicken, we all went back together, my mom and myself loves to be at kitchen gossiping she, told me about the importance of spices, that little is more you should be balance on eating food and cooking food, everything requires balance and scientific method while cooking, if we think about diet and fitness, we will surely control ourself in everything. Many days past I was in home for about almost 14 days, I was happy with my family, I and Saurav talked at night about our lives and how much we are attached to each other, it's been time now that I have to return back to Bangalore for work process so I was really excited to meet him after 14 days.

CHAPTER 9

It was Monday early morning my dad told me, "After completing the book work come and stay with us for months because it is required that you be at home and it's your home Kuhu just come when you are done, ", "Yes dad, I will come soon, my mother always send me cooked cake, it is a gesture of love, mom dad never scolded me while leaving it's the pain of leaving me, they are always like that come home, we will see you forever, the bond with the child and parents are the most underrated bond, but it is the most purest form of love but the respect between each other is the most humble, kind and lovable form of gesture in any relationship and it is the best form of love. I hugged my mom and dad, outside the airport and told them, "Don't cry I will be back home fast just after completing my book in 14 days I will be back in next 14 days I promise". I was excited I was going to see Saurav now, I was just too happy, "Esha don't worry I will pick you up at 11 am, I am coming after giving leave application at office, So, it was an early morning flight but my mom and dad came to drop me at airport, but more than anything else I was not willing to leave them, it was just that I wish not to go, I just promised that I will come back soon. After 3 hours of journey I landed back to Bangalore, I was super excited, that I was going to see him, "Saurav where are you I just landed, when you will come to pick me up, please come fast, I'm just very tired come fast baby, I miss you please come fast, I was super excited to see you".

"Yes baby I am on way coming just go take out the luggage bags, just go freshen yourself, I'm just reaching by then". Everything was all okay I took my bag, I was excited and I saw him, "Hii my chubby chubby, how have you been I missed you so much, but you know na I spent time with my family members so that I don't feel bad that I don't give time to them". I saw him, he smiled but I could sense, he was not happy from within last time when I saw him, the hug what he did to me, everything was all different, there was something mysterious, maybe he was just tired of working alone for some days and he was not with me for so many days that's why may be I was feeling like that.

In those 14 days when I was not meeting him, I had went to ISKON temple at my place, I prayed in front of the divine purity of love, kindness and respect that the love between Saurav and me should never break, I waited for that Maha Aarti, I prayed there for almost 1 and half hours I read about the bond of purity between the two individual souls and how Radha Krishna is the divine union between individual self and the universal self. I was so confident that this time, nothing can break my bond with Saurav, nothing no matter time, no matter career or work life imbalances or anything, I was just super confidence that okay I am not with him but God will protect our love between us and it will not change, everything will be warmth between us, no one wonder we will be together I just want to be with him. Only the divine power would know how much intensity I prayed to them, that please I know I have committed a lot of mistakes in my life; a lot of problems and issues is there in between us, but God and Goddess please bless me with your blessings that we might not get separated from soul. I prayed to God that he is so beauty, the symbol of warmth and bondness between us just prevails like your strong presentation of love and devotion. I know ISCON is just so special for me, I am a very workaholic person myself but when it comes to relationship values, I really want my love to be not less than the love what Radha does to Krishna. My love for Saurav, is not like that he visits or be with me daily, I don't want him to be with me every time but I just want that when I think about him just the smile in my face prevails, there is nothing a guide to love him, but his face, body, soul everything I get attracted to. If might my eyes was not there, if he was nearby me, I would know its him. Once, I did not knew he was coming from office meetings to meet me, I was just standing on road side in tea shop, having my favourite cup of tea and biscuits, it was late night around 10PM, I did not knew he was coming back from Pune after work, he was going to surprise me but I have no knowledge about it. He was just passing by my back, I did not saw his face neither I knew it was going to be him, he was wearing a black pant and black plain shirt, he was totally black from top to bottom, it was all dark just the little bit of tea shop was opened so, it was so sure that nothing was visible but in case of him nothing matters to me, his presence only will make a difference, no matter I am able to see him or not. While I was enjoying my cup of tea, all of a sudden a strong feeling I felt a strong intensity that I know this guy, my body was just so chilled, in my mind only one thing came Saurav, I had not seen his face till then but my whole mind and body knew it was him, I looked back, he had walked little bit more forward, I could see, he was going towards my building, but was not sure that it was him. I thought if it is him, he will definitely call me if I'm not at home, so I completed having my tea. After 2 mins, my phone was ringing, I picked up, "Esha why are you not opening the door I am waiting outside", I really smiled, as I knew this is going to happen for me LOVE is just warmth and being in peace with him as in life, everything is just not easy so love is all about just being there for.

Finally he arrived at the airport, I hugged him, sat in car just beside him, he kept my luggage at the boot of the car, I was so happy to see him, I got back my Saurav, the one and only my Saurav nobody else will come in between us, I was so sure about it. Likewise last time he was not talking to me inside the car, I thought he was just listening to the music of car, so I also preferred not to talk that much I thought we will talk whole day, as he informed me that he took leave for me. I was super excited I got time for us, and off course sex (I smiled little bit). But on the contrast, it was strange while I was flirting with him, he was not happy genuinely, it was a fake smile that time I felt with a strong feeling that honestly, he was not happy at all. For me this is strange, that he was so attached to me before, everything was so warmth in between us but suddenly he was not taking things lightly, he was ignoring things, and I could see he was really serious on things this can be seen with his behaviour. While he was driving I kept my hand on his hand when he was changing gears, it was a romantic gesture for him always, I knew this before but this time, it was little bit strange, he suddenly removed my hand and said, "Baby let me drive with focus, don't disturb me while driving, you should be cautious while driving so why are you distracting me just enjoy your music na please". I was just feeling weird, he was just so being rude to me, he was scolding me, for touching him, it's so strange, the one who always hugs me is telling me now don't touch my hand, maybe I am overthinking it, but his behaviour was disturbing me so much, just the little bit of strange feeling was coming to me, just not good it was him, I know him from 2018 and it's a long time knowing someone, for me it's my friend just the casual feeling was also not there is a little bit of strong feeling that something is just not right, you know that sixth sense was coming, but he never showed me that he was upset.

We came to Bel circle, his favourite place, he enjoyed his whole college life here, I thought maybe this could cheer him up."Baby let's eat here please, I am feeling hungry, please just let's go to your favourite place, Gilly's Resto bar New Bel Road"."Esha you might be tired let's go directly baby home"."Saurav please please|" "Okay we will have lunch ok let me take left turn towards, New Bel Road, don't worry we will go". New Bel Road is actually the main commercial roads near ISRO (Indian space Research organisation) and its popular landmark is Ramaiah Memorial hospital, so many nearby college students go there for just chilling but for college students, it's a refreshing place and I know Saurav is really having old college memories from this area, so I thought why not go and cherish it, everyone knows it's not the road which have huge impact on you but it's the story behind it or what was memories and emotions which leaves a deep impact on your heart and brain thus, then you don't wish to vanish it. I did not really thought anything I just saw him that he is with me why not go as a friend and let me refresh his mind on his favourite place, and I would also get chance to visit it as it was my first time. I just wanted him to have a good time, he took leave so I wanted him to just take little bit of break from his daily stress routine, make him little bit light on his life, he would feel happy and I thought maybe I am overthinking as we did not stay connected that much when I went so that might be the reason just so I thought lets be together as a friend and make things little bit calm and just chilling like a best friend. Sometime I just want to hug him as a whole but I stop myself thinking that he might feel I am always wanting romance with him but actually, he misunderstood me, I find myself protected, cared and it's all enough when he is with me.

We reached that favourite place of his, he smiled little bit, I felt relief that finally I could keep him happy as my main goal is always making him happy. As we entered the bar was mostly not so filled I thought we are too early or what, we went to ground floor first it was mostly empty so the manager asked us to go up in balcony and have some quality time as they told its peace up you can enjoy view and have a good time."Baby lets go up then", "Yes Saurav, Ok come lets go". We both went up and really saw a beautiful scenery, we could everywhere all greenery it was really beautiful, so peace and the tables were so vibrant in colour blue colour mix with grey it was so lively and the sunny day it made us little bit positive from inside. Saurav take my hand and let me sit inside first and then sit just opposite to me, this is why I like him, he is so gentleman, whatever might be the reason he, will never ever stop being so caring. I wonder why he is like this, there is so much going inside his mind, I guess he is disturbed but still does not stop caring me and just being with me."Esha lets order, what you want baby ?" "Babe just order something what you wish for, wait let me order|"."Sir can you please take our order" I asked the waiter. He came and asked, "Yes mam you say"."Sir just please one chicken biryani and one mutton curry with 2 glass of mango beer and one water bottle"."Sure mam". Saurav smiled and asked me, "Baby biryani ? You are so tired but then also you wanted to come here all of a sudden what happened, Is everything okay?" "Yes chill Saurav, just wanted us for some time, you tell me what you did all these days without me. Did you went to Pune for work ? Tell me na baby I am curious now". At first Saurav smiled because biryani and mutton curry is his favourite and the only reason why I ordered it is how much he loves mutton curry though he knew it that I never consume it, it's all he will eat.

"Esha I missed you so much; happy to see my buddy, How is everyone at home? How is Suku, baby?" "Saurav everyone is okay babe it's us now tell me, How is Abhijeet and Varu and all of your friends, how you enjoy boys parties Haan without me, I know you might enjoyed a lot these days but I will come and irritate you baby now."He laughed loudly and told Yes; I know this my bad days are back. We were talking and joking a lot just talking as buddies and then the food was arrived so, Saurav took the spoon and served me first little bit of biryani and took mutton curry and while serving only he was smiling and saying, "Oh my mutton curry finally you are here after so many months my favourite food at my favourite place with my best Esha super good". The honesty and friendship what is between us really matters to me that whatever might be the reason, he don't lie to me, I am strong enough to hear from his mouth anything but I don't wanted anytime that something I get to know from outside I wanted to hear everything from his mouth this makes a difference to me. You know when Saurav started to speak up, he told about a story that, "Baby you know we all went too Bumblebee Indiranagar, Trisha was too drunk, Rudy took his hand on her mouth so that she did not vomit on us, we all were stuck in the lift around 2 am coming back home, we all were scared whom she will vomit, Trisha was crying sorry Guyz, I am not able to control my vomit my head was paining, Abhijeet and I was looking at each other, when she is going throw all drinks on us; Mayank and Rudy was trying harder that she don't might vomit on us, Rudy was standing just in front of Trisha, so that she might does not vomit on us, but just reaching fourth floor, she pucked everything, Oh shit everyone was like, Why you did on lift, we were just reaching our flat, and we all laughed Rudy took her too room cleaned himself, cleaned her and took responsibility of her.

I, Mayank and Abhijeet was looking at lift so we got to know cleaning this is our job, Mayank and Abhijeet was drunk but they were cleaning the lift with Lizol and all and I was laughing seeing them as they were fighting for this stupid thing that who is cleaning the lift more properly so. So, I could not stop laughing really. This happened the next day when you left, I was just about to leave for Pune at work, but this happened so at night everyone was just chilling and laughing what happened while Trisha was sleeping, we all had that boys conversation so these funny things took place when you was not there baby, I missed you that time in the time of happiness. I know when Saurav becomes calm he started to share a lot to me.

I asked him, "baby are you done or you want to sit more, we sat down there till around more than 2 hours", as he took holiday, he could at least give time to me have lunch otherwise from many days we did not eat together so I was excited and now we will go home and take rest.

CHAPTER 10

The strong sunny winds are coming to me while he was driving I felt relief that he is happy now, everything was calm and I could see smile on his face, he is just driving and saying me, "Why so traffic babe, just go buy some juice and stuffs". I went and bought things whatever he told, we reached home after half and hour. After reaching home, I just took shower for refreshment, by that time he made coffee as we reached around 5 pm and as he is addicted to coffee so, he sat down and was having coffee with cake (little bit serious, thinking something). I came out with shower my hair was all wet, I was wearing a frock, just came to him and kissed him, on his neck, he was like,

"baby why are you so romantic today", "Why only boys have fun (while laughing), I was actually happy to see him not romantic but I was happy while seeing him. But Saurav was little bit stressed as if he wanted to say something, I thought he would kiss me, I came back after so many days so I thought he might be little bit in mood as when I was there he texted me daily that I miss you and please come fast baby, I thought he wanted me to come so early, and surprise him. But his behaviour was little bit suspicious, he was with me but then also I could sense his presence, but his mind is somewhere else. I hugged him, and said, "Okay you work, I am also going to work little bit then, you don't want me so I am going to work". I worked till 9 PM, completed my writings as during my home also I was working daily so it was on the urge of completing it, my whole story was again something different those 4 people saw the killing of that child on the hotel, the police suspected it and took the mother of the child but actually it was not the mother it was his lover who killed it but I wrote the book with deep crime thoughts for me it was also little bit difficult because my genre was romantic poets so I was really tensed. Is it going to be a good one or bad, my first ever crime novel, I was in deep thoughts and tension about completing it. I wanted my readers to love it and accept my new content and just enjoy the thrill, murder mystery, suspense scenes and I would able to be at up to the mark and people should like it, I was just praying to God that this should get good response, my work is to put all the efforts and rest is in the hands of audience so all the best to me. While pending down the last paragraphs I just thought to make it better and more better rest let's see, fingers crossed so finally my book was completed with more than 300 pages with 15 Chapters let's see the response, I did challenge myself I hope I put all the hard work and efforts and tried that I would impress my team and they accept my writings. I worked till 9 PM, Saurav called me for dinner, he asked me to make some rotis, he made aloo bhujiya and dal a traditional dish of Jharkhand and Bihar side, we both find it light and relaxed. After dinner, Saurav told me that he is going for a little bit of walking and off course ; I knew where he went so I thought let's do something till he comes. I thought we should just chill in bed, it was around 11 PM so, I thought let him come we will spend time as I know from next day, he will back to work and we will do nothing.

Saurav was very serious the whole week we don't do sex as he is super busy and finds himself so tired of work that whole weekdays we only work and chit chat together and sleep only on weekends we took time for ourselves, our quality time our lovvy dovy moments are only for weekends, he is really strict towards his job does not want to be disturbed and procrastinated on weekdays but I thought lets cheat today, he took leave so just take a chance. I just waited for him, he came late around 11:30 I thought why, he is so late, my mood was all spoiled, I thought leave it, he came and hugged me, and suddenly kissed me I was just standing near my table keeping and organising my manuscripts for the final print outs, and said, "Baby I wanted to say something to you from many days, I am not able to say to you I am really sorry I am not able to speak to you"

"Saurav What happened Yaar? Why you look so stressed out? What happened baby? Do you want to say something just tell me please, now you are giving me tension. From that time from airport I am finding that you are little bit disturbed just tell me why you are so tensed up don't think about me just tell me what happened babe? You know right that I am your girlfriend but also, I am your best friend just tell me what is disturbing you I can't see you so tensed up like this. You know I love you more than anything else so you can tell me what happened nothing will change anything between us okay. Just love you baby (I kissed him back and hugged him), No matter what Saurav, I would always be Mrs. Esha Shailendra Saurav, I am planning to be with you, thinking about marriage and settlement so when I thought this is it, then no matter what is the issue I will stuck with you like a fevicol, for me, marriage is not something, I took wows in front of everyone or priest, for me marriage is just like the love what Radha ji did to Krishna selfless love, the day I kissed you and started loving you, feeling for you that what was the day when I was actually married to you, marriage is a connection of two souls and so I am already married to you, I was just going to do the rituals so that everything gets into place ; my love and your love becomes one that's all, Baby tell me now, I promise I am here speak now ",

"Baby I kissed someone, you left me I was very upset that day when you left me, the next day after at office party, I kissed someone from school, I am sorry I know it's the biggest mistake I did and you won't accept it I know, I am sorry I was upset I wanted to distract myself I went to meet my friend, she liked me from school so she started to kissed me after dinner, and I did not stopped her, and when she kissed me things turned into one by one and I did mistake I am really sorry baby, I know am guilty but please don't leave me, you know I committed mistake, I know nothing can fix it but please, right now don't leave me, I know nothing can fix this, I cheated on you, but truly I don't want you to leave me please, wait, try to listen out things". I was shattered from top to bottom, at first, I just could not digest this, I thought he might be joking, I could not hear anything I was not able to analyse what he just spoke to me, my whole world just shattered everything got changed in this just few moments, my environment, my life got stuck, I just got angry on him, "Saurav please just go now I can't see your face now, please sleep outside, I want to take rest, I have a meeting tomorrow, please you go" (he went out at dinning space). I closed the door, and started to cry, the whole night, I cried, my tears was just not stopping I don't know how to react to this, I was just crying and crying the whole night, I don't know when you love someone, the mistake if he did also, why you get so much hurt that, you wished, it should not happen at all, I wish this time would never come in my life, I was just interested in one thing, I love him and I am not ready to get separation right now, I cried a lot(slept by mistake as I was too tired the whole day, I was travelling so because of tiring I slept). The next morning I took shower, got ready as I have to go to office and submit my manuscript for publishing so I went to kitchen, made a coffee for Saurav and some bread omelette and left it in the kitchen, I came out saw he was sleeping on the sofa, I could see he also did not slept the whole night, I did not spoke anything to him, he was asleep, I wrote a note on paper, and kept it on table that I am going to office| While I was in metro I was thinking, why it happened to me, what could be the reason, I was not able to give time to him as, I got busy in completing my project, or the reason that I was not being with him, what was the reason behind it, I am not able to calculate what was the reason behind it, what caused this to happen, the whole ride I was thinking about why it happened and all, what to do next as this was done by him and now what to do, we both are in this relationship, so in today's world we have to face together and fight for being one, no matter what, any challenges will come, the whole mountain will come but I will try to sort every problems which will come in my life. I know this is the most difficult, phase in both of our lives, its going to break everything in between sus but I thought, I am not able to break ties with him, he is not just part of life rather he is my life. I was too much hurt rather than being angry I was hurt of whatever he did, I could never ever forgive him for this, never I know I could not forgive him for this cheating, cheating for me is the end of any relation, breaking up of truth, trust, communication everything leads to destroy of any kind of relationship between the two. At office I submitted my manuscript and told everyone, that start the procedure for printing in next 15 days please fastrack everyone please, I want to release this book in next coming month, I want it to be on Amazon after 20 days, just fastrack everybody, I will launch in next 20 days that's for sure. I was part of all meetings lead by marketing team, we talked about the cover design, took more than 3 hours for work discussion, and at lunch time I saw message from him, "Baby please come home after work, I ordered prawn biryani for you, your special lunch go and have it, please come home after work, I'll be waiting for you, we need to talk please come babe, nothing else I want please just come". After whole day got over all work got over, I went back home, as soon as I came home, I saw him, he was drinking, I thought, this not the right time for me to talk, he was fully drunk, I ordered some burgers for both of us, I gave him burger and went to bed and did not wished to talk, for many days I did not spoke anything with him, though he was at home, I did not talked to him, I just ignored him, 5 days passed away, I did not spoke a word, I daily made breakfast for him and leave to office but I was not talking to him, I just did not wanted to come back home, my mind was totally fucked up knowing these things.

In a relationship, if any one person will also make mistake the whole bonding and relationship suffers, it's not a problem of an individual now it's the problem and difficulty which has to be faced by both person. Relation will have to face many problems but in the bad times you stood together stand with each other, be one this is the most critical thread of any relationship, if you both pass the bad times together but still chose to be one this is it you both are now whole, integrated and satisfied with together, it is now a balanced relationship, it has to be both who have to put efforts and make it work. Relationship is a work which requires communication, understanding, bonding and mostly respect and honesty only these will make a happy warmth between the couples.

At Saturday, I came back after work, I was just going to my room, Saurav came in front of me and hold my hand and said, "Baby please talk to me at least, from one week you are not just saying anything you just leave before my wake daily you come home late, don't talk anything to me, you just take your food and go inside room and lock yourself from inside. He took my hand (in total frustration, anxiety and tension and fear in his face was clearly visible) and said,

"Beat me, slap me baby, please burst on me, why you are not reacting anything babe, Why you should speak to me na atleast, how many days this is going go be we cant be living like this for lifetime and if we are planning to be together, we need to sort this otherwise it is going to be too difficult Esha, What you want from me, I should leave this place and go, okay I am going now then forever, I won't return if this is what you want, what you want God Damit tell me please what you want, I am done with all this now, take the keys, I am keeping in the table, I'm leaving now, I am also done, I don't understand what you want from, you want me or else I should leave you. What you want from me, tell me I should go, right now I am going, this is your place, stay here, seeing me finds you more in pain, grief, devastated, and depressive, angered then; okay I am going you don't need to be out whole day because of me, I am the one who is culprit and I am the one who should leave the house not you baby. I just love you right, you know I just got fucked up, and my all mind, I should have controlled myself, just tell me what to do otherwise I am not able to focus on work, you decide please, it's your decision off course, I am not forcing you to stay but I know you are the one for me. I know you love me more, than I love you, we are totally different, but at the end you are my comfort in life and if you are just not there with me, I am just not me, yes there is work stress, I want to increase my LPA more than 50 you know that, I am just fucked up babe, don't go right now, please I wish things to be just go down". I never said this to you, I know because I'm less expressive than you I could not speak about my feelings, thoughts whatever I wish in life I am not so vocal about it but today I am saying this to you, "Please for us just stay".

"You know Saurav, for me it's more difficult but I am not able to leave you, that's true I don't know but I am not able to just say this that get out from here, I know this should not be forgiven but for me without you I am nothing. I am just not able to leave you and neither wish you to go right now. You know when everything I lost, my man, my ambition my goals I was struggling hard to get back in track ; I knocked the door I asked for help from you just please come and help me, I thought at first you will not help me, but you came and hugged me tightly and helped me get out of my pain and grief, not a single day I am not grateful for you, every day, each minute I am lucky that you have been there for me on each and every step (tears was in my eyes while saying), you are the one because of whom I am standing with a strong mind, whatever I am just my happiness everything is you. You know whenever you use your green citrus fresh pocket perfume for men, and then spray on me at first I got angry on you always but then when I smell your body perfume on myself I get happy that you are connected with me the whole day, these small things of yours connect with me makes me happy whole day and when I come back home, I sleep on your chest just the touch of your skin, this embraces our love and trust, and I don't think anything I am just so relief that I am with you the comfort mind that you are here nothing is going to happen to me that level of cool mind and the trust I always did to you, the deep sleep I use to go as I was free from all worries all because of you, everything just vanished in just one minute, I can't imagine the separation from you, but you just broke my whole world, why you want to stay here, I promise I can't love anyone with this much intensity I did you but Baby you never valued me you think, I'll never leave you and go so you just think I am accepting everything and if you would have been in my place, you would have never forgiven me."

"Esha try to understand, it was just a mistake, how can I prove that I want you, what do you want me to do tell me na, she was just a mistake I am sorry".

"I can wait for you till many years Saurav but I can't just sorry, how much handsome you are, anyone can get married to you just leave me please, I am not willing to talk to you about anything right now please. If you wish to stay you can definitely stay here, it's your place too, I know you will be leaving for your masters soon so I will be okay, no need to think about me, I always knew you had to go to USA, University of Southern California, so it's okay I am done please I know some months are there and you will be leaving this fall so leave this conversation I think you should prepare yourself for your masters and I should focus on my work, I am having deadlines for my submission so I have to finish it, you want to be with me, stay with me I have no problems, just be here and focus on your goals, I am sorry baby I can't accept this, Good night (went to him) hugged him and kissed him and bye take rest babe many days you have not slept so please go sleep".

Saurav came to me and said, "Baby can we just go for a walk please just us no stress talking please I insist, I just want to cherish our moments right now, just once please"."Really right now after all this, baby okay it's your wish so okay". We both went down for a walk, he asked me, "Baby where is the keys for my scooty, have you seen it?"

"For what Saurav, we are just going for a walk right?" (I was really pissed off, confused and tensed)

"Come with me ", he took my hand locked the door, we walked together to my gate, he took the scooter and told me to sit in it."Where are we heading to Baby". It was little bit late I asked him, "Is it necessary to go now babe ?" "Don't worry Esha I am here with you, no matter what I am here so I just want to show you something". He started to drive scooty, we started heading to where I really did not knew about it.

CHAPTER 10

The night was so dark, moon was little bit deemed, and the sky was really clear, Bangalore weather was altogether so good at nights, cool breezy winds and I was in scooty, though my mood was so hurt, angry and fucked up. But he was driving, I was sitting at the back, my hands was in his shoulders, I could see, he was driving calmly, but still, his whole mind was on road, he was at little bit speedy, I could see, he was heading towards Baiyappanahali metro station, for I was just thinking why he is going to this route, but I was shocked this route is always filled with cars at daytime but now it was just so calm and cool, it was really wow | Suddenly I realised, we are at Pai layout, I asked, "Saurav why are we here, you know I don't like this place at all."

"Baby chill I am just reaching out why you are shouting at me."It was around 12 midnight, I was shocked, he spotted near a tea shop, "Really tea right now, Are you out of your mind ?"

"Don't ask so many questions just take two cups of tea till then, I am going to park the scooty at my house". It was all peace I could only see some people sitting in balcony and enjoying the calm environment, it was 16E Cross it was just near his flat, he told me to wait. The tea shop at the entrance of his lane and it was having a dead end as it was just near the railway tract but still at night the lane is just so calming, and peaceful and the vibe is just so romantic just like him. He kept the scooty at the parking space and came back and just smiled at me and told, "Don't think anything, just walk with me"."Right now we are here at your place, suddenly what happened?"."Uff you can never switch off your mouth right, Please bear with, me and let me chill little bit" (Saurav was cooling down his mind).

The road was so calm, only both the sides the streetlights was on and at left side the long trees was looking for so warmth and its reflection on the road was making it more wholesome. We completed both and enjoyed our tea, it was really refreshing, I was still upset, but the breeze was making me think about something, I was not at all angry but I was just enjoying the moment first time, I was enjoying peaceful nights.

There was only one street light which was glowing and sparkling like anything, I was just thinking it's the best time, we both together as always and I don't want anything more now.

Saurav suddenly took my hand, "What are you doing baby?" I asked him. For a surprise he really bend his knees at the middle of the 16th E Cross pai layout at midnight, took my left hand and put inside his palm and asked me, "Will you be with me forever? Just like this".

"Are you proposing me right now, after all this". (Fully confused)

"I am just asking the love of my life to stay with me, like this forever.

I will accept no/yes anything what you wish to say I am not going to say anything baby it's all your call".

"Where is my ring? I asked him (my eyes was starring him), I could see the Saurav transforming into a man whom I always wished for in all my dreams. I was seeing him, he was in his knees, his eyes was filled with love for me, the fear for my reply, the gentle way he took my hand, he was just in his shirt and track pants, I thought I would be getting a good proposal but like this; he in his track pants, it was all of a sudden for me.

I could not control tears, is it truth everything? all of this was in my mind, everything was just going so forward to me."Miss Esha Marshall will you able to jhelo me for the rest of your life ? Will you just never leave no matter whatever will happen? I am not saying this in fear, but you deserve to know all this baby.

From the day we are fighting, not a single day you forgot to make a breakfast for me, you were ignoring me, but still with lots of pain and anger for me, a lot of tension, with lot of hurtness you still cared and loved me a single damn fucking day. You know what I don't know you loved me more or I do to you, but this question should remain a question, we both should love each other with more and more each day with lot of more intensity, increasing everyday with the rest of our life. You are my reality, whenever I need you, you just come gave me your shoulder and came running to me and hugged me. Will you be mine forever, Soch lo abhi hi chance hai fir you can't change it. Baby say little bit fast my knees will pain then (he laughed).

I said, "No fast you should sit like this more you made me wait for this so much, I was patiently waiting for this". (controlling my laugh in front of him, trying to be serious in looks) so, that he finds me more serious in his thoughts. First time he spoked so freely about his feelings, I really liked it, he spoken to me these words, I was shocked totally out of blew my mind got a 100-volt shock equivalent to one electricity shock, I was very happy. (I made him stand and hugged him very deeply)

"You know what Baby (my eyes were in tears), you really changed me from day one we met you are fighting with me. But there is a kind of huge attraction and attachment with you, there is a kind of calm and a bit practical. You connect with me so easily and you are my support system, because of you, I now understood what is the real meaning of love. I love you baby and its no body except YOU."

"So is it Yes ?"

"It was always Yes for sure Saurav"

"Chalo lets go to my home from today which is our home".

"For the first time, he opened the flat and I entered the 401A Flat, he told me to go to his room and rest; his roommates were sleeping. I opened the door of his room, it was all white and it was so cleaned, that my eyes were like so Shailu (nick name called by Esha only) was really not joking that time.

"So, I bought Xplore Strawberry condom your favourite Esha (while he was laughing and standing at the entrance and starring at me with great intensity).

He came and hugged me very tightly, "Thankyou Babe, I am so happy that officially you are mine"."Love you Shailu" (giggling with him and enjoying). Stop teasing me Esha otherwise I wont let you sleep the whole night, lets sleep baby, Sweet Dreams.

Actually, love is not about the time period or how much years you spent with your partner, it's the love who gave you self-confidence, hope to stood up again and who always been your backbone who explains you

Stand for yourself and around him your Self will only grow more and more in all the toughest time. I am just thankful that I got to experience such a beautiful and pure feelings on my journey called life.

www.ingramcontent.com/pod-product-compliance
Lightning Source LLC
LaVergne TN
LVHW041844070526
838199LV00045BA/1430